Camouflage

ALSO BY MURRAY BAIL

Homesickness

Eucalyptus

Holden's Performance

Camouflage

STORIES BY

Murray Bail

PICADOR
FARRAR, STRAUS AND GIROUX
NEW YORK

www.picadorusa.com

Picador® is a U.S. registered trademark and is used by Farrar, Straus and Giroux under license from Pan Books Limited.

For information on Picador Reading Group Guides, as well as ordering, please contact the Trade Marketing department at St. Martin's Press.
Phone: 1-800-221-7945 extension 763
Fax: 212-677-7456
E-mail: trademarketing@stmartins.com

The stories in this book were previously published by Text Publishing in two separate collections: *The Drover's Wife and Other Stories* and *Camouflage*. "Healing" has appeared in *The New Yorker*.

Russell Drysdale's painting *The Drover's Wife* is reproduced courtesy of the National Gallery of Australia, Canberra.

Library of Congress Cataloging-in-Publication Data

Bail, Murray, 1941–
    Camouflage : stories / by Murray Bail.
      p. cm.
    ISBN 0-312-42087-0
    1. Australia—Social life and customs—Fiction. I. Title.

PR9619.3.B25 C36 2002
823'.914—dc21   2001053254

First published in the United States by Farrar, Straus and Giroux

First Picador Edition: June 2003

10 9 8 7 6 5 4 3 2 1

Suppose a mouse were to run across a stone. Just count each step it takes. Only forget the 'each'; only forget the word 'step'. Then each step will seem a new movement . . . A flickering will begin. The mouse will start to flicker. Look about you: the world is flickering (like the mouse).

—notebooks of A. I. Vvedensky (1904–41)

CONTENTS

Camouflage

The Seduction of My Sister

My sister and I were often left alone together. She was younger than me, about eighteen months. I hardly had time to know her, although we were alone together for days on end, weekends included.

Our father worked odd hours at an Anglo-American tobacco company. And our mother, she had a job at Myer's. Ladies' shoes, manchester, toys and whitegoods were some of her departments. She worked Saturday mornings, and there was the stocktaking. She put in a lot of overtime, working herself to the bone. Some nights our mother arrived home after dark, more like a widow in black than a mother, and passed around meat pies from a paper bag, one for each of us, including our father. Otherwise we were 'left to our devices', our mother's term; I heard her explain to a neighbour over the fence.

For a long time I took little notice of her, my sister, always at my elbow, in the corner of my eye. Whatever I was doing she would be there. More than once I actually tripped over my sister. She seemed to have nothing better to do than get in the way. She said very little, hardly a word. She and I had different interests, we were interested in totally different things, yet if I was asked today what her interests were I couldn't say. Tripping over her once too often or else wanting nothing more than to be left alone I would turn and shout at her to go, get lost, even giving her a shove; anything to get rid of her. Half an hour later she would be back, all smiles or at least smiling slightly as if nothing had happened.

My sister was skinny, not much to look at. She had short hair in a fringe, and a gap between her teeth. If anybody asked what colour eyes I could not answer, not exactly. There was a mole above her lip, to the left, almost touching her lip.

Taking an interest in something or standing near a group she had a way of holding her mouth slightly open. I can't remember a single thing she said.

The mole could have by now transformed into a beauty spot, I've seen them on other women. Brothers though are supposed to be blind to the attractions of their sisters.

Our father had a small face, and although he didn't himself smoke the odour of fresh tobacco followed him like a cloud, filling the passages of the house. I don't know about him and our mother. About their happiness or contentment even it was difficult to say. When our father spoke it was to himself or to his shoes; he hardly looked at our mother. In reply she would say nothing at all. Sometimes she would make a strange humming sound or turn to us and say something unrelated. Arriving home after standing behind a counter all day our mother looked forward to putting her feet up. After the table had been cleared our mother and father often went over the various budgets, income and outgoings, gaining some sort of pleasure or satisfaction from the double-checking. If he saw us watching our father would give a wink and make a great show of scratching his head and licking the pencil.

It was a short street, the houses dark-brick from the thirties. Each house had a gravel drive and a garage, although hardly anyone had a car, and a front hedge, every house had its box hedge, except directly opposite us, which was an empty block, the only one left in the street. It was surprising how long it remained empty, swaying with grasses, lantana in the left-hand corner. Who in their right mind would want to live all day looking across at us? Our father winked at us, our mother taking a breath, not saying a word.

It remained then, a hole in the street, a break in the hedges, in the general tidiness, an eyesore to more than one.

Nothing lasts, that is true; it goes without saying. Nevertheless, the morning we woke up and saw pyramids of sand and a cement-mixer on the block it was a shock to the system, the builders more like intruders than new neighbours, trampling over habits and feelings.

Slowly, then rapidly accelerating, a house took shape out of the disorder and commotion; I would have preferred it to last forever, so much there to follow, to take in and assemble in my mind. I can't speak for my sister.

Instead of retreating at right angles to the street like any other house, including ours, it was positioned longways, parallel to the street. It caused our father to give a brief laugh of misunderstanding. He called it 'The Barn'. Instead of bricks the colour of lamb chops which slowly turn brown, ours, it had cream bricks of a speckled kind, and grey tiles on the roof instead of the painted corrugated iron of ours.

I came home one afternoon late to see my sister standing at our front gate as always, waiting for me; only, I could tell by the way she was twisting one leg around the other she was talking to someone.

The Gills had moved in, their doors and windows wide open. Gordon withdrew a hand and introduced himself. He was their only son; about my age.

The house inside was still smelling of paint. In his bedroom he had a stamp album and cigarette cards scattered on his desk, and merely shrugged at the model aeroplanes suspended from the ceiling, as if he had lost interest in them. We went from room to room, my sister and I. In the lounge Gordon demonstrated the record-player which opened on silver elbows into a cocktail cabinet. Shelves and glass cabinets displayed plates and bowls and porcelain figures. From another room a clock chimed. Now and then Gordon stepped forward to explain something or take it from our hands, then returned to the window, answering a question or my sister's exclamations. Across the street directly opposite stood our house, stubborn, cramped-looking. It was all there to see.

Mr Gill put down a lawn, bordered by roses, not ordinary roses, but dark roses, and stepping stones of slate to the front door. Mr Gill had a moustache, the only one in the street, and a strong set of teeth. From the moment they met he called my father 'Reg', and made a habit of dropping it with informal gravity into every other sentence, sometimes flashing a smile, which pleased my father no end. 'Do you think, Reg, this weather's going to hold?' And, if he was in the middle of something, pruning or striding around to open the car door for Mrs Gill, who remained seated looking straight ahead, he'd glance up and with a single nod say 'Reg', and return to what he was doing. Even this pleased my father.

It was our mother who suggested doubts. 'No one,' she was scraping the plates, 'is like them, not in this street. They might as well be from another planet.'

With his wide shirt open at the neck our father put his finger on it. 'They're all right,' he smiled, 'they're extroverts.'

Our mother always looked tired. I wondered why she kept on working, what on earth for, but she went on almost every day of her life, Saturdays included, at Myer's. Through the store she bought a washing machine and a Hoover, demonstration models, otherwise brand new. In turn the store made a new fridge possible, the varnished icebox ending up in the garage, along with our father's hat-stand, tennis racquet in its press, and a God-forsaken electric toaster. Chimes were added to the front door, a new letterbox smartened up the front, father's idea, displaying our number in wrought iron beneath the silhouette of a Mexican asleep under his hat.

Taking a tour of our house one afternoon Gordon barely said a word. A floorboard kept creaking; I noticed the light was yellowish and the walls, carpets and chairs had a scruffy plainness.

In no time we were outside by the fig tree where I searched around to retrieve something. 'That'd be a hundred years old,' I pointed with my chin.

To demonstrate, my sister in her cotton dress shinned up into the first fork. Grinning, she looked like a monkey, I could have clocked her one. I glared and hissed at her, but she took no notice, which only gave the impression she was used to such cruel treatment.

I steered Gordon into the garage, my sister scrambling down from the tree, not wanting to be left out. Our mother and father never threw anything away. Poking around I held up things I thought might be of interest, waiting for his reaction. And Gordon too began examining things, the old tools, tin boxes, our mother's dressmaker's dummy from before she was married. He squatted down, my sister alongside. It was Gordon who came across the gramophone records still in their brown-paper sleeves. Reading the labels one by one he carefully put them back.

I thought he was being polite.

'Tell you what.' I had an idea. 'You go and stand on your front lawn,' I glanced up at the sky, 'and I'll send a few of these over the roof at you.'

'What for?' He remained squatting.

It took a while for the penny to drop.

'See if you can catch them or something, I don't know.' I had to push him. 'You stay here,' I told my sister.

Before Gordon could change his mind I yelled out from the back of our house, 'Coming now!' And in a simple quoit-throwing motion sent up in the half-light the great Caruso singing something mournful in Italian. It soared above our iron roof, the disc, and in a moment of dark beauty tilted, almost invisibly, and hovered like the tenor holding a high note, before returning to earth. My sister and I both had our mouths open. I reached our gate, sister alongside, to see Gordon waiting on their patch of lawn, hands in pockets, suddenly give a hoarse cry as the black 78 brushed his shoulder and thudded into the lawn beside him.

Hardly able to run, laughing too much, I crossed the street. 'What d'you reckon?' I gave him a shove. 'It almost took your head off.'

Picking up the record Gordon wiped it with his sleeve.

Nobody spoke. He could have gone one way or the other, I could see. I took another look at him, my sister gaping at one of us, then the other. I ran back to my position, not saying anything.

I sent over *Land of Hope and Glory* and, before he could recover, *The Barber of Seville*, followed by the *Nutcracker Suite*. I had others in a stack at my feet when the street lights came on, and Mrs Gill began calling in her musical voice, 'Gor-don.'

Anyone could see he was not suited for sporting activities. The sloping shoulders, the paleness, even the hang of his arms—unco-ordinated. Yet the following night Gordon was in position early, pacing up and down, looking over to our side.

I waited for it to be almost dark. To my sister I called out, 'Look at me. See how I do it. If you like, you can have a go later.'

I began throwing and threw, in quick succession, one musical disc after the other. They were hard to spot in the night sky, that of course being the idea, their closeness suddenly revealed by a faint hissing near the face or the back of the head. They were lethal. Quick reflexes were necessary. And concentrating hard and working on his technique Gordon took everything I sent at him. He used his feet, swaying from the hips. With each throw of mine the better he became; and so his confidence grew. It wasn't long before he began in a lackadaisical manner grabbing at the black shapes as they came down at him or past him, managing to pull down in mid-air one in three or four, without saying a word, even after leaping with an arm outstretched, thereby putting pressure right back on me on the other side, sister looking on. Some I tried sending in low or at unexpected angles, anything to catch him off balance.

My sister had moved to the front gate where my throwing efforts could not be seen, where instead she could observe Gordon facing up to the onrushing discs. For a while the pressure began to get to me; I had to talk to myself. The heads of Mr Gill's prize-winning roses were severed; another night, a disc I gave too much wrist kept on going above Gordon's shout and outstretched arm and smashed against the mock louvred shutters Mr Gill had bolted to the wall, showering Gordon with fine-grooved shards. Almost before he could recover I sent a recital of a legendary pianist, forget his name, Jewish, who died just the other day: wide of the mark, wrong grip, it sailed through the open window of the Gills' lounge room, my sister and I waiting for the crash of all that bone-china which never came. There were moments of ordinariness, moments of poetry. Simplicity, I realised, produced elegance, not only in the throw, in Gordon's response as well. One night, Melba, collector's item I'm told, sliced through Mr Limb's new telephone wires next door which fell over Gordon's face and shoulders like string. Gordon froze, my sister too; hand went to her mouth. They didn't have a clue about electricity, Gordon and my sister were not mechanically minded. Realising he was not about to be electrocuted Gordon kicked the wires and some of his embarrassment aside and went back to his crouch.

Engrossed in our separate tasks we hardly spoke, every throw presenting a different set of problems. It changed Gordon, it opened him up. He'd come around to my side early, rubbing his hands as if it was freezing, my sister looking on.

'One of those records the other night,' he followed me into the garage, 'boy, was it funny.'

I was sorting through the few that were left.

'You ought to hear *Laughing Gas* one day. It had the old man rolling on the floor.'

Along with *Little Brown Jug*, the Satchmo selections and *Sing, Sing, Sing* it would have been our father's. Our mother, I was told, had a singing voice. Always with a grin hovering at the ready our father had a taste for imaginary honky-tonk playing; he made the cutlery jump on the table, sister and I watching. I began putting the remaining 78s back in the trunk.

'What are you doing?' Gordon grabbed my shoulder. He began reading the labels. 'What about these?'

At that moment I wanted to pause; something felt out of place. Twice he whistled he was ready. I stared at my fingernails, waiting to think clearly. A few houses away a dog barked, and someone was trying to start a motorbike.

It took less than a week, if that, to go through the remaining 78s, and when they were gone we tried chipped or broken discs, until it was too difficult to throw or nothing was left of them. Even so, when I realised the entire collection had gone, a feeling spread in my stomach of corresponding emptiness.

I dismissed Gordon's suggestion we continue, using saucers, his idea of a joke: saw him nudge-nudging my sister. She was hanging around us, always there. A glance at her scrawniness could trigger irritation in me, I don't know why. Anything he said she'd listen, mouth open in that way. I would have said, look, scram, buzz off; words to that effect. I was about to, when Gordon reached for something wrapped in newspaper under the bench, and we squatted, sister too, I could see her pants.

Lifting it out I untied the string.

'Eek!' She clutched at him.

I held up a fox with glass eye.

'O-kay,' I swung experimentally. 'This'll do. What's the matter?' I stared at my sister. 'I can throw it.'

Before she married, our mother dressed up for special occasions, little hats, veils, dresses consisting of buttons and tiny flowers. One photo in the album has her on a shopping spree with her mother in the city, each with a cheesy smile, like sisters. Shortly after, she met our father, I forget where. Near the back door I was adjusting my feet, getting the balance right. I swung a few times, began again, swung once more, again, sud-

12

denly letting go with all the smoothness I could muster, the centrifugal force of the lopsided fox hop-hopping me forward like a shot-putter.

Leisurely, the doglike shape began flying, its tail outstretched. At the chimney it somersaulted in slow motion against the night sky, appeared to set course, and with snarling teeth nosedived straight for Gordon across the street, chatting to my sister. At her cry he tried to swerve. The fox followed, sinking its fangs into his throat, as he rolled on the lawn.

A fox is pleasant to hold, weighted at one end, a living thing. I never tired of sending it over, enjoying the accelerating moment of release, then running up our drive to follow its twists and turns, flash of orange tail, its Stuka-dive forcing Gordon into the acrobatics of a goalkeeper, exaggerated for my sister, looking on. 'Improvisation is the mother of invention!' I heard him call out. My sister swallowed anything. At the same time she had a frivolous side; I could imagine reaching our gate to find her parading in front of him, fox draped over one shoulder, hand on hip for him.

As mentioned, the houses each had a hedge, except the Gills', which had the picket fence, leaving the house naked. The Gills didn't seem to mind, on the contrary. Every other night the lights would be blazing, more like an ocean-liner than a house, the rest of the street as dark as the sea. The rectangle of illuminated lawn appeared as a billiard table, the beds of roses, shutters flung open, car in the drive all added up to a welcoming, optimistic air. After the loss of the fox I sent over a rubbish-bin lid, glittering chassis of a crystal-set, tennis racquet in its press, other objects so poor in the aerodynamics department they barely cleared the roof. They were not adding anything; I was beginning to lose interest.

The card table had a way of setting its legs in mid-air, to make a perfect four-point landing on the Gills' lawn; but that only happened, I think, twice.

Our father would begin picking his teeth with a match, and for the umpteenth time tell us what a time he had, the best years, working with cattle in the outback, before he married, only ten months, but enough to deposit slowness in his speech, a corresponding glaze in our mother's eyes, and a green trunk full of Aboriginal weapons in the garage. I had forgotten they were there. Gordon was holding the boomerangs in his hand, authentic tribal weapons, not the tourist kind.

'You might as well put them back,' I said. 'They're too dangerous.' When I turned my sister was already skipping around to the front, Gordon at her heels.

'Listen, will you?' I crossed the street. I grabbed my sister. 'You're not going to watch me, right?' I felt her squirming. 'Then you'd better keep your eyes open. In case someone's coming, that's why. These things,' I sounded prim, 'could kill someone.'

Gordon was in no doubt as to the serious turn the game had taken. Boomerangs were altogether different from the grimacing masks and decorated shields from New Guinea displayed in the room Mr Gill called his 'study'. If one caught him in the face it would have been curtains. We knew, Gordon and I, my sister too; Gordon began going through his stretch exercises. Instead of hesitating, let alone calling a halt, I was gripping the boomerang at one end.

I gave plenty of elbow: let go.

By the time I reached the street the boomerang was ahead of me. Gordon on their lawn was shielding his eyes. My sister had moved from the gate to be alongside. The mulga blades came swirling out of the fading light in a fury, seeking him out. Keeping his eyes on it, swerving and ducking at the last moment, he avoided being hit, just. He was impressive, I'd have to say. From then on the vicious insistent things kept coming at him, at the strangest angles, finding him in roundabout ways, where least expected, side-on without warning or from behind. While I had never underestimated his confidence, I think I underestimated his abilities in general. He had a certain course of his life marked out, even then. He would always succeed where I would not, I could see. In the end my life became something of a shambles. His would not.

Gordon wore his father's yellow driving-gloves and was grabbing at the boomerangs as they flew past, my sister clapping encouragement whenever he managed to pull one down. Keen eyesight, reflexes played their part, fair enough, knowing which ones to leave, sure; but as I watched I began to find his way of crouching and twisting, particularly in the region of his hips, distasteful. He displayed a fleshy alertness I found off-putting, just as when he received a given object and turned it over in his hands I saw his arms were precisely the pale arms with black hairs I found unpleasant, repulsive even. I have always had trouble with such hairy arms, my sister didn't seem to mind. Every night her job was to whistle or cough if a motor cyclist appeared or a pedestrian, such as Mr Limb, a bachelor who lived next door, deciding to stretch his legs, it's all she had to do; otherwise I was throwing blind. But she was more interested in warning him, Gordon, crouching there on the slippery lawn; more than once letting out a cry, which may well have saved his skin. I had to cross the street and tell her to pipe down, we didn't want the neighbours coming out. If she didn't we'd have to stop, it would be the end. As I laid down the law she began to blink, I could see she was about to cry. Gordon nearby examined his elbow saying nothing.

Gramophone music came from the Gills' open windows, men and women moved in the brightly lit rooms, now and then a man leaned back laughing his head off. This flat boomerang felt longer on one side, inscribed with dots and whorls. Without thinking too much I flicked it, perhaps that was it, for as I ran with it up the drive the thing hovered like a lost helicopter blade above our chimney, before returning. Slipping on the gravel I ran back just as our father stepped out the door.

'Bloody crow!' he waved over his head. 'Did you see that?'

It clattered into the fig tree, but by then our father had cocked his ear to the Gills' party noise.

'Benny Goodman,' he gave a bit of a jig, 'at the Carnegie Hall. Hello, how's Gordon tonight?'

Gordon pulled up panting, sister alongside. As soon as our father went back in our mother began getting stuck into him, listing things missing in him.

'Think.' Gordon was shaking me. 'Where did you say it landed?'

'I'll find it in the morning. Don't worry about it.'

His answer startled me. 'Put it off and never find it again. That'd be right.'

Already up in the tree my sister dropped it at his feet. Wiping it with his handkerchief Gordon held the flat blade up to the light. Whatever he saw pleased him, for he lunged with both hands at my sister as she passed, ignoring me.

No matter how hard I tried I never managed to make another one return. And when the trunk was empty, even of fighting boomerangs, which Gordon explained were never meant to be thrown, the problem again was finding something to send over. In this and other matters Gordon revealed a singlemindedness I never had. Gordon knew what he wanted, usually had a fair idea. What I thought hardly worth the effort he invariably thought the opposite. Already he had a sureness in summing up the other person, then no longer taking them into account.

Anything I could lay my hands on I was letting go. I found all sorts of things we did not want. Nothing ever meant much to me. Even today I am casual about possessions. With people too I come and go. In this I resemble my casual father, who in the end disappointed people, my mother and others.

In a single night I sent over a pair of suit trousers, striding across the sky, a row of coat-hangers, textbooks I would never open, wooden lavatory seat. I watched as every copy of *Life* presented to me by an amateur photographer uncle changed hands, the history of the postwar world turning over like a newsreel. Patterns form without anyone being fully aware, I see now. Our mother wore the same shoes for a week and a half, our father never changed his hat.

Electric light bulbs lit up the sky, followed by the first fluorescent tube; our pop-up toaster another time trailed its

plaited cord. Problems of a technical kind: it took several at-
tempts to hurl the standard-lamp over, a ceremonial spear. The
electric radiator made the journey, the single red bar describing quite fantastic arabesques, catching Gordon talking in
the shadows to my sister by surprise. When occasionally she
skipped over to my side, expressing interest in what I was doing, I could see she was itching to get back to him and whatever he was saying, on the other side. I set the American alarm
clock for seven o'clock in mid-flight, and as it began ringing
Gordon reached out and silenced it with one hand. I chucked
half a dozen eggs, we kept fowls in the backyard, rotten tomato, a navel orange, another joke, Gordon collecting it on
the neck. He said he confused it with the moon, but he was
talking to my sister, I saw them. And for the first time my sister turned on me, 'That's going to leave a bruise,' as I ran up
arranging a country grin, in the manner of our father.

Eventually we come up against things said by others
which cannot be explained, not at the time. The night our
mother talked about 'taking in ironing' made us laugh our
heads off, my father and I; my sister too after a glance, our father laughing the loudest, almost choking, at the same time
placing his weakened hand on my mother's arm, which she
pulled away. 'Your mother sometimes comes out with all kinds
of rubbish,' wiping the tears from his eyes. At the table my sister sat demurely. It made me look twice, our mother too. The
few jokes I cracked in her direction, not worth repeating, she
ignored. The usual family racket we made she seemed to find
irritating, which in turn irritated us, at least our mother.

From the beginning, I began to see, I was doing all the

work. To Gordon I suggested we change positions. Operating in darkness near our back door I could do my bit with my eyes shut, whereas on his side light was absolutely essential, he pointed out. 'Without proper light I've no idea what's coming my way.' I'm at the receiving end, let's not forget, he actually said.

Besides, he pointed out, we have each attained a degree of efficiency in our respective roles. 'Isn't that right?' he said to her, alongside.

The pale ironing board in flight reminded me of the loose skin above my mother's elbow. Difficult to send up and over it was more difficult still for Gordon receiving, a matter of manoeuvring desperately to get side-on to the torpedo-shaped thing. At the same time Mr and Mrs Gill stepped out for a night at the theatre or somewhere. By the gate I watched Mrs Gill, fox over one shoulder, although the night was warm, flash my sister a smile. 'So this is Glenys?' I heard her say. After that she made a point of saying hello, Gordon looking bored, as Mr Gill strode around to open her car door.

To get my sister's attention Gordon sometimes touched her with his foot. Other times, talking to me, he'd drape an elbow over her shoulder. In turn, my sister remained still, no longer jumping about. He subscribed to American magazines and gave her books to read.

Birdcage, oval mirror reflecting the clouds, a perfectly good floral armchair.

The smallest things amused my sister. She had what I would say was a childish delight in small and modest things. It was one of her attractive sides. And yet when I sent over things chosen for her she reacted as if they had dropped from the sky into his lap, as if it had nothing to do with me, on the other side.

I submitted silver coins when I had some to spare. 'We're down to our last shekels,' I called, the coins shooting across the sky as falling stars.

It was she who pointed them out to him, I could hear her cries. It would have been their appearance amongst the stars that caught her eye, not their value; I can't answer for him. As always Gordon hardly said a word; I mean to me: I could hear him murmuring to her. Mostly you never knew what he was thinking; he never gave much away. Vase of flowers, inner-spring mattress, dustpan and brush. By the time I'd reach their gate he'd still be talking to her, my sister taking in whatever rot he came out with. It had been the same with me. So practised had he become he'd merely extend an arm and take whatever I'd sent over or simply move a step, holding her by the waist, a provocative move.

She was out of my hair, I was no longer tripping over her, a good thing; at the same time, I felt great rushes of irritation at the way she transferred her attention lock, stock and barrel to him, in that trusting way of hers, mouth slightly open. If our mother saw two people with heads together they were 'as thick as thieves'. And more than once she said, 'No one likes anyone whispering.'

A large oil painting from our mother's side used to hang in the bedroom, a summer landscape, on canvas. It aquaplaned into multiples of parched hills and fat gum trees. Gordon received it with open arms, my sister helped him lower it to the ground, and listened as he launched into a lecture, pointing out the strengths and weaknesses of the composition. After examining it and wiping it with his handkerchief he pronounced it too fragile to travel, my sister nodded in agreement.

In the way the boomerang came back over the roof it was only a matter of waiting before our father's expression returned to one of smiling slightly. Mr Limb, next door, used to say, 'I don't have a hobby or a pastime,' and as he reached retirement, 'Most of my life has passed, and now just when I need it I don't have a hobby or a pastime.' The subject of early retirement occupied his mind so much he suffered excruciating headaches; he took days off from the work he no longer enjoyed, on medical advice.

Even then I felt sympathy for Mr Limb. I don't know what in the end happened to him. The umbrella jerked open and parachuted down, ironic cheers from Gordon's side, ashtrays were never used in our house, nest of tables, mother's, and our father's tan suitcase opened its mouth and dropped a sock on the telephone wires.

From my side in darkness I would hear Gordon's voice, followed by her laugh. Rolling pin tumbled over, dusted with flour. They would have trouble finding the knives and forks. I no longer bothered rushing around to see how the latest thing was received. We were going through the motions, little more. Only later do we realise something of value has slipped away. Whatever had been worth the effort in the beginning was coming to an end; a feeling I would recognise in later years.

I squatted near the garage, my sister, Gordon at her elbow, rummaging through what little was left.

Embroidered tablecloth, their idea, didn't make the distance; I could have told them that. At any given time there is only a limited number of ideas of value, I wanted to say. And before long we exhaust them as well. I remained squatting, watching them. If one of them went somewhere the other followed. I was left alone, to one side.

That night when my sister came skipping around to my side I thought she was coming around to my way of thinking, whatever that was.

Instead, she had a suggestion, and as I listened I felt my father's grin beginning to run amok; but she was looking away strangely and speaking vaguely.

Thinking the thing she suggested was going to be the last I got to my feet, not at all laboriously, and went inside. I came out with it rolled up.

So many things passed through my hands; nevertheless, I found it necessary to use all my skills with this one, and wondering whether it was her idea or his dispatched, after some difficulties, my sister's favourite party dress. I could follow its progress, walking up our gravel drive. Billowing from the waist it elbowed gently past the chimney. And in its determination, oblivious to me or anybody else, I glimpsed my sister there and in years to come. She would always be determined, always there, her way, while I felt within a heavy casualness, settled and spreading.

Whatever Gordon was expecting it wasn't this. Directly above him the translucent dress began descending, flapping gently at the edges. Not sure whether to grab it with both hands, or perhaps deceived by its slowness, the slow hip and narrow waist movements, he was caught wrong-footed. The white cotton dress smothered him.

I waited for my sister to rush forward and help, as she had

all along, but she looked on, not lifting a finger, letting Gordon disentangle himself.

From the gatepost if I glanced across the street I would see Gordon's outline, kicking gravel, my sister discussing something. I had almost forgotten what my sister looked like. The dark bulk of the house now came between her features and me, obscuring aspects of her personality even. Out of habit I hung around near our back door. From inside the kitchen I heard the soft thudding of our mother ironing, occasionally the murmur of our father.

Things at least seemed to be steady there, I remember thinking.

At the sound of her voice, my sister, I stood up. Gordon was one step behind, both hands in his pockets, pursing his lips.

My sister whispered again. Why the whisper? I wanted to ask. Facing her, I noticed a rushed, wide-open expression I hadn't seen before.

Still I didn't say anything. After a while my sister went inside, leaving us. He and I stood there. Gordon glanced at his watch. When she came out in her white party dress he stepped forward.

'How am I?' she asked in a small voice. She was speaking to me. The gap opened between her teeth as she smiled.

It allowed me to place my hands under her arms. She was much heavier than I imagined, I could feel the soft swell of her breasts. She allowed my hands to remain there; she was my sister.

I looked at her once more. 'Are you all right?' I was on the point of saying, 'Is this what you want?' Other questions reached my tongue, but her body had surrendered, and by then I had taken an interest in the whole technical question; I began gathering momentum. In an almighty heave-ho, putting my whole body into it, I let go.

Trust and optimism were always her main characteristics. Now she tilted her chin, and dog-paddled among the stars, then clasped her hands more like an angel than my sister. Putting her trust in me she was now putting her trust in him. I concentrated on the mole near her lip, a point of focus, until it too began diminishing, along with the pale hopes of her body, gap between teeth, fringe, balanced on one foot, listening: all this blotted out by the chimney.

I heard Mr Limb's cough. He was setting out on his evening walk, for health reasons. I felt so much around me slipping, accelerating, beyond my grasp; for I was left with nothing. Running from my side towards the light I began calling my sister's name, to where she had gone.

The Drover's Wife

There has perhaps been a mistake—but of no great importance—made in the denomination of this picture. The woman depicted is not 'The Drover's Wife'. She is my wife. We have not seen each other now . . . it must be getting on thirty years. This portrait was painted shortly after she left—and had joined him. Notice she has very conveniently hidden her wedding hand. It is a canvas 20 × 24 inches, signed l/r 'Russell Drysdale'.

I say 'shortly after' because she has our small suitcase—Drysdale has made it look like a shopping bag—and she is wearing the sandshoes she normally wore to the beach. Besides, it is dated 1945.

It is Hazel all right.

How much can you tell by a face? That a woman has left a husband and two children? Here, I think the artist has fallen down (though how was he to know?). He has Hazel with a resigned helpless expression—as if it was all my fault. Or as if she had been a country woman all her ruddy life.

Otherwise the likeness is fair enough.

Hazel was large-boned. Our last argument I remember concerned her weight. She weighed—I have the figures—12 st. 4 ozs. And she wasn't exactly tall. I see that she put it back on almost immediately. It doesn't take long. See her legs.

She had a small, pretty face, I'll give her that. I was always surprised by her eyes. How solemn they were. The painting shows that. Overall, a gentle face, one that other women liked. How long it must have lasted up in the drought conditions is anybody's guess.

A drover! Why a drover? It has come as a shock to me.

'I am just going round the corner,' she wrote, characteristically. It was a piece of butcher's paper left on the table.

Then, and this sounded odd at the time: 'Your tea's in the oven. Don't give Trev any carrots.'

Now that sounded as if she wouldn't be back but, after puzzling over it, I dismissed it.

And I think that is what hurt me most. No 'Dear' at the top, not even 'Gordon'. No 'love' at the bottom. Hazel left without so much as a goodbye. We could have talked it over.

Adelaide is a small town. People soon got to know. They . . . shied away. I was left alone to bring up Trevor and Kay. It took a long time—years—before, if asked, I could say: 'She vamoosed. I haven't a clue to where.'

Fancy coming across her in a painting, one reproduced in colours like that. I suppose in a way that makes Hazel famous.

The picture gives little away though. It is the outback— but where exactly? South Australia? It could easily be Queensland, West Australia, the Northern Territory. We don't know. You could never find that spot.

He is bending over (feeding?) the horse, so it is around dusk. This is borne out by the length of Hazel's shadow. It is probably in the region of 5 pm. Probably still over the hundred mark. What a place to spend the night. The silence would have already begun.

Hazel looks unhappy. I can see she is having second thoughts. All right, it was soon after she had left me; but she is standing away, in the foreground, as though they're not speaking. See that? Distance = doubts. They've had an argument.

Of course, I want to know all about him. I don't even know his name. In Drysdale's picture he is a silhouette. A completely black figure. He could have been an Aborigine; by the late forties I understand some were employed as drovers.

But I rejected that.

I took a magnifying glass. I wanted to see the expression on his face. What colour is his hair? Magnified, he is nothing but brush strokes. A real mystery man.

It is my opinion, however, that he is a small character. See his size in relation to the horse, to the wheels of the cart. Either that, or it is a ruddy big horse.

It begins to fall into place. I had an argument with our youngest, Kay, the other day. Both she and Trevor sometimes visit me. I might add, she hasn't married and has her mother's general build. She was blaming me, said people said Mum was a good sort.

Right. I nodded.

'Then why did she scoot?'

'Your mother,' I said thinking quickly, 'had a silly streak.'

If looks could kill!

I searched around—'She liked to paddle in water!'

Kay gave a nasty laugh, 'What? You're the limit. You really are.'

Of course, I hadn't explained properly. And I didn't even know then she had gone off with a drover.

Hazel was basically shy, even with me: quiet, generally noncommittal. At the same time, I can imagine her allowing herself to be painted so soon after running off without leaving even a phone number or forwarding address. It fits. It sounds funny, but it does.

This silly streak. Heavy snow covered Mt Barker for the first time and we took the Austin up on the Sunday. From a visual point of view it was certainly remarkable.

Our gum trees and stringy barks somehow do not go with the white stuff, not even the old Ghost Gum. I mentioned this to Hazel but she just ran into it and began chucking snowballs at me. People were laughing. Then she fell in up to her knees, squawking like a schoolgirl. I didn't mean to speak harshly, but I went up to her, 'Come on, don't be stupid. Get up.' She went very quiet. She didn't speak for hours.

Kay of course wouldn't remember that.

With the benefit of hindsight, and looking at this portrait by Drysdale, I can see Hazel had a soft side. I think I let her clumsiness get me down. The sight of sweat patches under her arms, for example, somehow put me in a bad mood. It irritated me the way she chopped wood. I think she enjoyed chopping wood. There was the time I caught her lugging into the house the ice for the ice chest—this is just after the war. The ice man didn't seem to notice, he was following, working out his change. It somehow made her less attractive in my eyes, I don't know why. And then of course she killed that snake down at the beach shack we took one Christmas. I happened to lift the lid of the incinerator—a black brute, its head bashed in. 'It was under the house,' she explained.

It was a two-roomed shack, bare floorboards. It had a primus stove, and an asbestos toilet down the back. Hazel didn't mind. Quite the contrary; when it came time to leave she was downcast. I had to be at town for work.

The picture reminds me. It was around then Hazel took to wearing just a slip around the house. And bare feet. The dress in the picture looks like a slip. She even used to burn rubbish in it down the back.

I don't know.

'Hello, missus!' I used to say, entering the kitchen. Not perfect perhaps, especially by today's standards, but that is my way of showing affection. I think Hazel understood. Sometimes I could see she was touched.

I mention that to illustrate our marriage was not all nit-picking and argument. When I realised she had gone I sat for nights in the lounge with the lights out. I am a dentist. You can't have shaking hands and be a dentist. The word passed around. Only now, touch wood, has the practice picked up to any extent.

Does this explain at all why she left?

Not really.

To return to the picture. Drysdale has left out the flies. No doubt he didn't want Hazel waving her hand, or them crawling over her face. Nevertheless, this is a serious omission. It is altering the truth for the sake of a pretty picture, or 'composition'. I've been up around there—and there are hundreds of flies. Not necessarily germ carriers, 'bush flies' I think these are called; and they drive you mad. Hazel of course accepted everything without a song and dance. She didn't mind the heat, or the flies.

It was a camping holiday. We had one of those striped beach tents shaped like a bell. I thought at the time it would prove handy—visible from the air—if we got lost. Now that is a point. Although I will never forget the colours and the assortment of rocks I saw up there I have no desire to return, none, I realised one night. Standing a few yards from the tent, the cavernous sky and the silence all around suddenly made me shudder. I felt lost. It defied logic. And during the day the bush, which is small and prickly, offered no help (I was going to say 'sympathy'). It was stinking hot.

Yet Hazel was in her element, so much so she seemed to take no interest in the surroundings. She acted as if she were part of it. I felt ourselves moving apart, as if I didn't belong there, especially with her. I felt left out. My mistake was to believe it was a passing phase, almost a form of indolence on her part.

An unfortunate incident didn't help. We were looking for a camp site. 'Not yet. No, not there,' I kept saying—mainly to myself, for Hazel let me go on, barely saying a word. At last I found a spot. A tree showed in the dark. We bedded down. Past midnight we were woken by a terrifying noise and light. The children all began to cry. I had pitched camp alongside the Adelaide–Port Augusta railway line.

Twenty or thirty miles north of Port Augusta I turned back. I had to. We seemed to be losing our senses. We actually met a drover somewhere around there. He was off on the side making tea. When I asked where were his sheep, or the cattle, he gave a wave of his hand. For some reason this amused Hazel. She squatted down. I can still see her expression, silly girl.

The man didn't say much. He did offer tea though. 'Come on,' said Hazel, smiling up at me. Hazel and her silly streak— she knew I wanted to get back. The drover, a diplomat, poked the fire with a stick.

I said, 'You can if you want. I'll be in the car.'

That is all.

I recall the drover as a thin head in a khaki hat, not talkative, with dusty boots. He is indistinct. Is it him? I don't know. Hazel—it is Hazel and the rotten landscape that dominate everything.

Life of the Party

Please picture a pink gum tree in the corner of a backyard. This is a suburban gum sprouting more green in the lower regions than usual, and a tree-house hammered into the first fork. A stunted tree, but a noteworthy one in our suburb. I live with my wife Joy and two boys Geoffrey and Mark in a suburb of white fences, lawns, and tennis courts. It has its disadvantages. On Sundays drivers persist in cruising past, to peer and comment as we tend our gardens. I wonder what their houses are like. Where do they live? Why do they drive around to see the work done by other citizens? Let me say I am concerned and curious about these things.

Last Sunday was a day of warm temperatures; pure pleasure, really. Tennis sounds filled my ears, and the whine of weekend lawnmowers. There was smoke from burning autumn leaves. I went down to the back of my yard, waited, looked around, and climbed to the tree-house.

I am forty-five years of age, in reasonable shape all round. On Sundays I wear brown shorts. Still it was a climb which was tricky in spots, and then as I settled down the house itself wobbled and creaked under my weight. The binoculars I placed on one of Geoffrey's nails; I moved my weight carefully; I surveyed my backyard and the squares of neighbouring houses. Half an hour remained before the party began.

On my left was Hedley's, the only flat roof for miles. He was out the front raking leaves. The sight of rubbish smoke billowing from that tin drum of his made me wonder at lack of thought. We had no washing on the line but was Hedley's act typical of a nonconformist, the owner of a flat-roofed house? It was just a question. It reminded me of his car (a Fiat), his special brand of cigarettes, his hair which was going slightly grey, and his wife, Zelda. Everything she did seemed to begin with Z. An odd game, but true. It was Zelda who owned the street's zaniest laugh, had zealous opinions on the best-sellers, and always said zero instead of the more normal nought or nothing.

In the next house I could see a tennis game. That accounted for the steady plok, plok and random shouts. I trained my glasses on the play without knowing the score. The antics of those people in slow distant motion was quite fantastic. To think that a wire box had been built to dart about in, to chase a small ball in, and shout. That was George Watkins. As director of a profitable girdle factory he has an inside story on human fitness. He's also a powerful surfer and when I see him walking he shouts to me, 'How you going, Sid?'

The first time I played a game with big Watkins he aced me and aced me in front of his friends and my wife. Invitations have been received since, but I miss the game to avoid additional embarrassment.

Across the street I could distinguish the drive and the side of Pollard's leafy yard. This is a Cape Cod type of house. As expected Pollard was there, walking up the drive, stopping at plants, hands in trousers, pausing, checking bricks, until he reached the footpath. There, he looked up and down, waiting for mail, visitors, his Prodigal Son, news of some description. He parades the width of his house, a balding figure with a jutting stare like the house.

To my right a widow lives with her daughter. The street was alarmed when Gil died—he seemed to be as healthy as any of us. A short time after, she had a swimming pool dug and tiled and can be heard splashing during days of hot temperature. From my position, as I waited, the waters were calm. Then I thought I saw a man there, lying beneath one of her pool trees, a solid hairy specimen, on one of those aluminium extension chairs. No? The glasses showed an image of some description. She is wearing slacks, and is blonde and nervous.

Finally, there was the house next door on my right. The binoculars were hardly needed: I was looking down into the weedy garden, and as usual not a soul could be seen. These neighbours are the J. S. Yamases. In three years I suppose I have seen them . . . a dozen times. We have not spoken yet. He has nodded, yes, and smiled, but not spoken. This indifference deeply offends my wife.

'It's wrong the way they don't mix in!'

'Why?'

'You can't live by yourself,' she says. 'What if something happens?'

That was her frustration as I remember it. Naturally enough, the Yamases' silence made them more and more discussed. The street kept its eyes open. Thinking about it: the Yamases have a private income; he could be a scholar of some sort; it could be, of course, that one of them is in shocking health, though I doubt it from what I sense of the place. He looks foreign, not Australian, and a fairly decent type.

At that time my yard was silent. Joy was at our beach-house with Geoffrey and Mark. I had said to them on Saturday night: 'Look, I have to duck up to town tomorrow.' Arriving, I arranged the place and made for the tree-house. I had raised the venetians and left the screen door open. We have lawn smoothing over most of our yard and concrete blocks form a path. (I used to say that ours was a two lawnmower house—one for the front and one for the back—until people took me seriously.) Halfway between the back door and the tree stands a permanent brick barbecue, tables and white chairs.

I had invited a dozen or so couples. On the tables I placed plenty of beer, glasses, knives and forks, serviettes, and under Joy's fly-proof net a stack of steaks, sausages and piles of bread rolls. Tell me a friend of yours who doesn't enjoy a barbecue on Sunday! From Geoffrey's tree-house I waited for the guests to arrive. Then a movement occurred on my left. A door slammed, floral dress fluttered, down my drive came Norm Daniels and his wife. With the binoculars I caught their facial expressions. They began smiling. He adjusted his blue short-sleeved shirt as they neared the front door.

I waited. The Daniels now came around the house, puzzled by the no-answer at the front, seriously looking down the drive; certainly bewildered. Had they arrived on the wrong day? Then, of course, they turned and sighted the barbecue all laid out, and their relief was visible.

Daniels was monk-bald to me as I stared down. He waited among the tables as his wife called through the back door, 'You-who!' She smiled at the fly-screen, then shook her head at the tables and chairs.

'Not there?' Daniels asked.

'They must have gone out for a sec.'

He looked at his watch, settled back, and began eating one of my rolls. 'Want one?' he asked. She shook her hair. Surrounded by someone else's fresh meat and utensils, she seemed uncomfortable.

Another car pulled up. Daniels went over to the drive.

'Down the back!' he called out.

It was Lennie Maunder. About fifty, he was as soft as pork, wore Bermuda shorts, and had a bachelor's lopsided walk.

'No one's here,' Daniels explained. 'They must have gone out for a sec. I'm Norm Daniels. My wife, Joan. Pleased to meet yah. We might as well hang around till they get here.'

They sat down and I couldn't catch all their words. It was a distraction trying to listen to them and watch for the next arrival. The word 'insurance' floated up to my tree, so I knew Daniels had started on occupations. They were not drinking at this stage, and when Frank and elegant Georgina Lloyd came down they seemed embarrassed, caught as it were, and stood up stiffly, bumping chairs, to smile.

Two more couples arrived, the men with bottles.

'Well,' Andy Cheel said, 'we might as well have a beer!'

Laughter. The sun was beaming. They began drinking.

The women were seated together, and pecked at the air like birds. I heard Frank Lloyd extroverting into Sampson's ear. Tiny for his name, Sampson was in a bank somewhere, and accordingly grey. Nodding, he said, 'This is right. This is right. Yes, this is right.'

Lloyd was in advertising and already into his third glass. He blew froth from the top of it. 'Ahhh,' he said, and half-closed his eyes.

The chairs were comfortable, the voices grew louder. Late-comers arrived. Norm Daniels and Lloyd realised they were friends of Ed Canning.

'Come over here, you bastard,' they said to him. Lloyd shouted, 'Who's the old bag you've got with you?'

'Oh, you!' said Canning's wife. She was quite heavy, but pleased with Lloyd's compliment.

'Have a beer,' he said, 'Sid's not here yet.'

And Bill Smallacombe, who was climbing at Myer's, arrived without his wife.

I had a brief mental picture of Joy. In bed one night she sat up and said, 'I saw Bill Smallacombe at lunch today with a young girl.' She fell back disappointed, full of indignant thoughts; a brown-haired concerned wife is my Joy. As I watched the party I imagined Joy submitting to the sun on the sand, breasts flattened, lying there keeping an eye on young Geoffrey and Mark. She must be satisfied with my career so far and is privately contented when I rush to town on business.

They were all there now, and the drinking had loosened muscles, floated the mouth muscles, wobbling the sincerities.

The perils of Sunday afternoon drinking! Ed Canning and Frank Lloyd had taken off their shirts, Lloyd's wife loosened her blouse buttons, familiar back-slapping occurred; laughter, so much laughter. I noticed the bachelor Maunder began stealing beer from someone else's glass. Bill Smallacombe drank heavily and kept going inside to use my lavatory. Clem Emery I could hear repeating the latest stock-market prices, and Sampson was complaining that his new concrete path had been ruined overnight by a neighbour's dog.

'What say we get stuck into the grub?' yelled Andy Cheel.

They all crowded forward, chewed on their words, dropping sauce and bones on the lawn, and briefly my name.

'Clear those bottles off the table, Ed, before they fall off,' said Canning's wife. She was wearing tight blue slacks.

Carrying four to each hand he lifted the bottles over legs, lawn, to dump them behind the garage. Two were dropped on the last load, and broke with an evil loudness. Someone called out, 'He dropped his bundle!' and they laughed and laughed.

Later, Ed's wife said, 'You should see their lounge!'

'Those curtains I didn't like,' said Georgina Lloyd. 'I suppose Joy picked them.'

'I've been with her when she's bought stuff that really makes you wonder,' said Joan Daniels.

'Where do you think they got to, anyway?' she asked vaguely.

By about half past four the party was noisy. This was emphasised when the Watkins' tennis game suddenly stopped. And from the corner of my eye I caught grey-haired Hedley next door creeping towards our fence. I waited. Hedley squatted down, peered between the planks at the goings-on. He hadn't shaved over the weekend, he twitched his nose, and at one stage scratched between his legs. For a good fifteen minutes Hedley spied before retreating. At his door he said something to his wife, and they went inside. Directly over the road, half-hidden by cars, George Pollard on the footpath faced the direction of our house. The other neighbours were either out or had decided to display no interest at all.

'Only a few bottles left,' Cheel announced loudly. 'Sid's got Scotch inside, but we'd better not.'

'Why not?' asked Lloyd.

There was laughter at that, and I had to smile.

Lloyd touched Canning's wife on her behind. 'You old bag,' he said. She allowed his arm to go around her neck as he lit a cigarette.

Lloyd later tried a hand-stand between two chairs, tricky at his middle age, and swung off balance, knocking chairs and breaking glasses. He landed on a pile of chop bones; he lay there sweating, his chest heaving.

'When are you getting your pool?' Georgina asked Clem Emery.

'Say seven weeks. We'll have a bit of a do one night.'

'Yes, yes, don't forget us,' others shouted.

Then Smallacombe came wandering down to the tree. He stopped right at the foot, kicked a tin, grunted, and loudly urinated. The others glanced vaguely. Sampson turned, but it seemed natural enough, relieving yourself against a gum tree on a Sunday afternoon.

Frank Lloyd, trying to balance a bottle on the hairs of one arm, was pulled away by his wife. 'Come on, darl. We must be off.' She called to the rest, 'We'll be seeing you.'

'Gawd, it's twenty past six.'

The Daniels moved out with the Lloyds.

'What about this mess?'

'She'll be right.'

Smallacombe belched.

'Leave it.'

My tree was draughty. They had me bored. I wanted them to go, to leave my place. Why do they linger, sitting about?

Gradually they gathered sunglasses, car keys, their cardigans and handbags, and drifted up the drive in a sad fashion as if they were leaving a beach.

At the gate Ed Canning stopped and shouted, 'I've never been so drunk in all my life!' It was a voice of announcement, sincere, and clearly loud enough to reach my tree. My binoculars showed middle-aged, sunglassed Canning rigid with seriousness after his statement. Canning, the manager saving for boat and beach-house; his wife had begun yoga classes.

Finally, there was the accelerating procession of shining sedans, saloons, station wagons, stretching past my house. Most of them I noticed had tow bars fitted. Canning, Smallacombe, Cheel, Emery, Sampson, Maunder, etc. One of them sounded his horn three, four times in passing. Was it Smallacombe? He was one of my friends. A stillness occurred, a familiar hour was beginning, lights flickered. And sliding down the tree I had to think about: who would have sounded his horn at me?

Zoellner's Definition

Definition. The action of determining a question at issue; an ecclesiastical pronouncement. A precise statement on the essential nature of a thing.

Name. The particular combination of vocal sounds employed as the individual designation of a single person or thing. To call a person or thing by the right name.

Zoellner's mother (whose name was also Zoellner) decided to call him Leon. His father preferred 'Max', but today on the birth certificate (and other records stored in cabinets in scattered buildings) he is identified as Leon—Leon Zoellner. In Zoellner's opinion the first name is an accessory only made necessary (perhaps) by the complicated world population. Whenever he thinks of the shape of himself he sees the word *Zoellner*. Like most people Zoellner is intrigued by the name which is used to identify him. In the telephone directory there was only one other Zoellner, an architect with initials R. L. whom he has never met. In Basil Cottle's *Dictionary of Surnames* he found only three names beginning with Z: Zeal, Zeller and Zouch.

Man. An adult male person. The human creature regarded abstractly. The spiritual and material parts of a human person; hence applied to the physical frame of man.

Zoellner has all the appearance of a man.

Face. The front part of the head, from the forehead to the chin; the countenance as expressive of feeling or character; a countenance having a specific expression.

Countenance. Appearance, composure of face; comportment.

He seems to be in mourning, or remembering something; Zoellner has that troubled vagueness. He seems to be listening intently; or he is waiting for something. The face has filled, rounded, folded and settled more or less naturally into the shape of those requirements. There is also the established persistence of his years. This can suddenly fix itself onto another face, or a foot, a metal object, a crowd, or a distant mountain. To be precise, Zoellner glances at these things too rapidly. He is keen. Strange though: looking in mirrors he has trouble describing himself. Perhaps Zoellner is tired of his familiar face, the disappointing lines, inevitable expressions.

Skin. The continuous flexible integument forming the usual covering of an animal body.

This is amazing stuff. The way it stretches and clings to the elaborate shape of Zoellner's ears, and other parts. Hair grows straight through it without a corresponding leakage of blood. Around the lips, however, it sometimes bleeds after Zoellner shaves. His skin is grey like the stone of city buildings. But looking at himself he sees a vertical body capable of locomotion, and none of the fine details of skin.

Eyes. The organ of sight, sometimes including the surrounding parts. The faculty of perception or discrimination of visual objects.

Positioned in fluid his eyes move in his head. Juggled by soft wires, apparently, they move freely without pain. His are the colour of wet nuts. Zoellner is positive: he would prefer to be deaf than blind. He has a stubborn wonder at sunrises, pigeons wheeling out from trees, waterfalls (and rain overflowing from blocked gutters), women's teeth, processions, huge wall paintings. Lately he has observed scenes of human misery, perhaps believing that the sight of horror and original emotions will reveal some of the foundations of knowledge. Zoellner has cried, but then most men have—or if they haven't they have felt like it. Zoellner reads. Most of the words produce the same movement: a man chases after God, or a white whale, gold, butterflies, women, evil men, etc. Zoellner wonders why they bother arranging these words. Other books he reads have a man chasing mysterious abstractions such as love, truth, power, respect, revenge and reality. Zoellner stands before a mirror and stares at every section of his face. His eyes are deceived. To touch his left ear in the mirror it is first necessary to find his right ear. It always surprises him. When not reading or looking into mirrors he imagines himself: he sees his shape walking towards him.

Spectacled. Provided with or wearing spectacles. In names of birds and animals having spectacle-shaped markings or appearance of wearing spectacles.

At certain angles the glass reflects light to such a sudden

extent that his eyes are invisible. The frames are brown plastic. Apparently they are necessary on his head. He removes them (he has this habit) and rubs his eyes. Zoellner's eyesight is getting worse. When it is tested he is asked to recognise letters from his language printed in rapidly diminishing sizes on a wall-chart. He is not asked to recognise pictures or mountains, or a forest, or a person's face.

Mouth. The external orifice in an animal body which serves for the ingestion of food, together with the cavity to which this leads, containing the apparatus of mastication and the organs for vocal utterance.

Usually this is horizontal and rather wide. Laughing, it twists and floats into a ragged circle; shaving, it is pulled into soft triangles; yawning, the slit becomes a black egg, and his teeth suddenly protrude into it. Zoellner's laugh is sudden and shy; it is both generous and genuine. He is amazed that the skin of his lips is softer and different in colour from the rest of his face. Often he breathes through his mouth. He drops food down the cavity, chews it, rolls it to the back, swallows the ball, repeats. Actually Zoellner has stopped enjoying the taste of food. With his mouth he touches the lips of others. He has noticed more than once that conversations between people are composed of questions. Thinking about this he compresses lips, making the mouth tiny, the lips themselves are crammed with tiny vertical lines.

Voice. Sound formed in or emitted from the human larynx in speaking, singing or other utterance; vocal sound as the vehicle of human utterance or expression. Sounds regarded as characteristic of the person and as distinguishing him from another or others.

He moves his mouth. It may be said that Zoellner curls his voice around his words; each syllable softly rolls into the next: his words are furry at their extremities: the sentences encircle invisibly from the air. A careful voice, not very loud. Perhaps he is cynical about death? That is what his voice sounds like. Characteristically, after producing a statement he will question it by adding, 'Mmmmm?' Lately he has lowered his voice in mid-sentence; those listening lean forward, rustling slightly. He soon questions others to check their statements—if there is room, if it is possible. His words seem to point. The letter in his language most suited to his voice is the circular *R*. So the words are offered. He hears the noise of his own voice. And then the words are gone. He thinks that spoken words are proof of the present, however temporary. But not the past; for the words, always visible, are departed, untraceable. And not the future; for Zoellner has not yet moved his mouth to restart his voice.

Cigarette. A small cigar made of a little finely cut tobacco rolled up in thin paper, etc., for smoking.

Protruding from his face is the white tube made by a machine, its red tip alive with silver smoke. Zoellner sends the smoke down his throat and allows it to fill his body. There it enters the narrowest places and trails throughout. Zoellner half-closes his eyes. He has filled the spaces in his body with a cloud. It pours out from his nose.

Tooth. The hard processes within the mouth, attached in a row to each jaw in most vertebrates except birds, having points, edges or grinding surfaces, for the biting, tearing or trituration of solid food. **Teeth**, pl. of TOOTH.

Zoellner does not feel comfortable (is always wondering)

when cracking nuts with his teeth, although his teeth are described as 'excellent' by several dentists. He has only five repaired areas, or 'fillings' as they are called: steel rods, lights and drills are aimed into the mouth, the holes filled with compositions of mercury and a tenacious cement. These filled-in areas are visible only when Zoellner yawns. Teeth are usually vertical; they have the appearance of polished bones. In the middle stand the largest; but of these the one on Zoellner's left is leaning across at an angle. The smoke of his cigarettes stains his teeth, the yellow most noticeable in the front. Zoellner has another habit: he closes his mouth and rubs the back of his teeth with the tip of his tongue. This of course cannot be seen by others, when the size, shape, colour and spacing of his teeth are also invisible.

Nose. That part of the head or face in men and animals which lies above the mouth and contains the nostrils.

The entrances to Zoellner's nostrils are partially blocked by hairs: they also protrude outside his nose. His nostrils are dark and rather wide. The nose itself is not noticeably large, but appears to be soft and porous, caused (perhaps) by the hundreds of tiny black holes. These can be seen when standing very close to his face. There is nothing extraordinary about his nose, and Zoellner himself rarely thinks about it. When blowing through his nostrils into a cloth to remove mucus he hears the noise (as do others): high, briefly loud, shuffling towards the end. Zoellner wonders why that is necessary. Other animals: do they remove mucus? Lying near a woman his chin is above her head. Looking up she notices (at that rare angle) his nose as an unknown shape related more to the peculiar stub of his chin. From there his face has an over-rounded graven appearance, alien and unattractive. Zoellner touches the nose with his hand.

Ear. The organ for hearing in men and animals. Its parts are the external ear, the middle ear and the internal ear, or labyrinth.

His father had voiced these words years ago. 'It is better that you have your ears cut off than never to learn what they are hung on your head for.' They are in fact auxiliary devices jutting from the sides of the head, partially obscured by hair. His ears are a deep red compared to the rest of his face. Zoellner sees that they are growing larger and more bulbous (bloated, bumpier) with his age. Still visible is the mildly circular labyrinth which must channel notes of an orchestra into his brain. These ridges also collect wind and dust. He listens to the actions and voices which surround him. It is necessary sometimes to turn his ear in the noise's direction. Noise, to him, seems true and solid, so true that it is unavoidable; it is, however, his most temporary indicator of time and reality. He touches his ears. Pinching with his fingers the flesh is insensitive.

Hair. The filaments that grow from the skin or integument of animals, esp. of most mammals, of which they form the characteristic coat.

The hair on Zoellner's head is falling out as if he had stood too near to some nuclear blast. In the mornings he wakes up with strands of rejected hair beside him. The edge of his hair is retreating towards the back of his head. Its colour has changed to muddy grey and gaps reveal raw skin. Worse, he sees that the whiskers around his chin are hardly growing. It is necessary to shave only every three days. He watches his face in the mirror. The hair on top of his head is cut regularly by another man.

Arm. The upper limb of the human body, from the shoulder to the hand; the part from the elbow downwards being the forearm.

The length and position of the arms establish his proportions. He thinks of other animals. When he stands his arms hang at his sides and bend out where portions touch his body, the tips of his fingers finish halfway between his groin and knee. His arms swing as he walks and he seems to lean forward for balance. He points, shakes hands; he has many times placed an arm around waists and shoulders of men and women. He leans on his elbow. Out of habit Zoellner uses his right arm more than his left. He writes with that hand.

Leg. One of the organs of support and locomotion in an animal body; in narrowest sense, the part of the limb between knee and foot.

His legs are now thin and pale, although invisible beneath layers of cloth. They carry him along the street in the evening. There his shape is seen moving between the immovable flat surfaces of buildings. He walks without thinking of his movement; one leg jerks ahead of the other. His mind has migrated his body to some other place, another complicated situation. And he seems oblivious. The street is coated in a thick yellow light.

Penis. The intromittent or copulatory organ of any male animal.

This swings in the air between his legs and settles itself horizontally as he sits, legs crossed. It can be seen as he urinates: the wrinkled penis, grey from lack of sunlight, as if a wet forest rock had suddenly been lifted from it. It feels insensitive in his two or three fingers, and during this, the draining of his body, he plays the fluid up and down in circular patterns. Zoellner watches. Inserting himself into the body of a partner, and striving, he is suddenly filled with profound melancholy and pointlessness, or he thinks of other women, fragmented problems, words.

Height. Measurement from the base upwards.

Zoellner without shoes measures 5 feet 6¾ inches. Metrically this is 1.68 metres. He also weighs 114 lbs. (51.71 kilos). At that height he is considered to have less than the desirable weight. Zoellner is regarded as an underweight specimen. He thinks more of the space he fills (approx. 7 cu. ft., or 0.1981 cu. metres) and the volumes of air he breathes. Generally he believes that measurements of distance (and time) are nothing more than arbitrary notches. His interest in space is, of course, another question.

Short. Having small longitudinal extent. Of persons: low in stature.

Zoellner is regarded as a short person. Most other persons would agree.

Clothes. Covering for the person; wearing apparel.

Zoellner covers his body in the same style of clothes worn at this moment in Pakistan, Indonesia, United Kingdom, Argentina, Chile, Germany, Quebec, Japan, Russia, Poland, England, Britain, etc., etc. This consists of shirt, necktie, trousers, jacket. Bodies of men are thus covered. There is little decoration in Zoellner's selection. He does feel however the cloth resting on the shape of himself. Beneath the material his body moves. He is walking down the street.

Age. A period of existence. The whole of ordinary duration of life.

He is 52.7 years old. This is a measurement linked to movements of sun and moon; beyond that, when Zoellner tries to feel the bulk of those years, it seems to be a blank period without edges: an imprecise mass. Zoellner tries to pinpoint his position in his own curving cycle. Where is he at this moment? He is compelled to judge his age in other ways: is 47 average? At that age he is past the middle, into a minority diminishing group. In his country 68.7 years is the average for death. Both parents have died: he is the member of the Zoellner family left to head towards it.

Reality. The quality of being real or having an actual existence.

Language. The whole body of words and of methods of combining them used by a nation, people or race. Words and the methods of combining them for the expression of thought.

Words. Verbal expression; used in a language to denote a thing, attribute or relation.

Healing

The quality of miracles has declined over the years. In Adelaide, a flat city, 'the city of churches', we all went around on bikes. I am speaking here of the mid-nineteen-fifties. My father, for example, rode an Elliott. It was a heavy machine, bottle-green, with leather cleaning bands rolling around the hubs, silver-frosted handlebars, and a seat sprung with two thick coils like hair curlers. My father with his grey face and his pitted bike clips: arriving home after the Magill Road climb he'd lean the bike under the grapevine and rest in the darkened kitchen with a sarsaparilla. It was a three-mile ride from where he worked. Yet—and I still believe this—our bikes and the pedalling past dry hedges somehow signify the period, the white light and optimism of the fifties. They fit in very well. The man across the street subscribed to the *Saturday Evening Post*. Things just seem more complicated now.

I said Adelaide is a flat city. Well, it is and it isn't. It looks flat on the map or from the air, but the wide intersecting streets contain an inbuilt slope of private dimensions, barely perceptible, often invisible to the naked eye. The city centre is located halfway between the sea and the perpetual purple backdrop, the Adelaide Hills. Our days consisted of coasting into the hot empty air, then pushing slowly back towards the hills. Magill Road here was a classic. It ran from the foothills to town, about four or five miles, straight and smooth, wide and harmless-looking. But try cycling up one day.

It was on Magill Road, about a third of the way down, that I saw the accident. I was one of the few.

Denis Hedley was considered a smart-alec. His bike was an Elliott, like my father's, but he had stripped it of the mudguards and painted the frame canary yellow and black. Around the wheel rims he'd painted a checked-flag pattern, which at low speed made old people dizzy. But its most conspicuous feature, and the thing that attracted ridicule, was a plastic aeroscreen he'd fitted, as on a racing motorbike, over the handlebars. The handlebars were black and horizontal, also like a motorbike's. Hedley had made them from a piece of pipe. Closer inspection—though we tried not to give Hedley the satisfaction—revealed other significant modifications. Every possible strut and clamp, even the bell, the wing nuts, and parts of the pipe frame had been drilled with holes to save weight. Hedley was too smart to talk much, but he confided casually one day that it gave him extra speed. And it was a blurred yellow-and-black fact that he dominated the upper reaches of Magill Road. Crouched behind the aeroscreen, legs pumping like wheels, Hedley would streak past trams and the small British sedans at thirty-five or even forty-five miles an hour and, reaching the Burnside Road intersection, which is near our street, would suddenly sit up and coast no-hands, sometimes combing his hair or scratching the small of his back. Then he'd brake, turn around, and laboriously climb back for another run. That was how afternoons were spent in Adelaide. He was thick-necked and of course had pimples and oily hair. He wore tight khaki shorts. Hedley was also known for his fourteen-year-old sister, Glenys. She had damp hands and a cowlike smile. She was the first girl in our district to suddenly begin wearing a brassière.

On this particular morning, my chain had come off and I was squatting down by the footpath. It was a quiet Sunday, hot; not many cars. As I say, I was one of the few to see everything. I happened to look up as Hedley went past. He had Glenys sitting sideways on the top bar—something I had not seen before. I could see they were going too fast. Hedley seemed to be struggling with the handlebars; Glenys was rigid, holding too hard. As they passed No. 1839 Magill Road—and oddly enough, I realise now, that was the year the bicycle was invented—Hedley's specially lightened frame appeared to buckle slightly, or fold, and because of his indiscriminate drilling this placed sudden strain on the brake strut. It snapped. It had been drilled too much. The back wheel then slid forward, throwing the chain and all hope of braking. What followed could only be called a chain reaction. The atrophied pipes of Hedley's bike, the drilled and countersunk sprockets and levers all began cracking and splitting, the little aeroscreen flew into the air, bits of broken metal and spokes fell off and jumped all over empty Magill Road like black sparks. The machine, no longer a bicycle, began weaving and contracting, approaching the intersection.

And then from behind came Boardman (that rings a bell!) on his mauve Healing. It was the latest model, with alloy guards, three-speed gears; Boardman was the local Healing dealer. As usual, he was riding with a lighted cigarette. With superb balance and strength for a thin man in his forties, with tremendous cool, he rode in close and, pedalling in top, lifted Glenys off and onto his serene handlebars. By then Hedley's tangle was almost at ground level, still sparking at high speed, and Hedley had one leg trailing. Again Boardman leaned over and down, this time more like a polo player, and grabbed Hedley by the collar, supporting the careering machine and halting further disintegration, while with the other hand he applied the chrome-plated brake callipers on the Healing, weaving to a halt across the intersection. At the last second Hedley lost his grip. His bike somersaulted in the clarity of that Sunday morning, snapped around the verandah post of Townsend's corner shop, and lay there in two or three pieces. Gleny's blouse was badly torn; I could see her ochre brassière. She immediately began swearing at her brother, and I realised she had grown up. She was no longer a girl.

Hedley stood there, one shoe missing, surveying the wreck. Boardman lit up another cigarette, waved, and rode off. I have not seen anything like it since. Boardman is dead now, and I don't know if they make Elliotts any more. Hedley and his sister must still be alive, grown up. My father is dead. A Shell service station has replaced Townsend's corner shop, and the intersection has been fitted with lights.

Portrait of Electricity

There were three guides. One did all the talking, the others nodded in agreement. They wore plain maroon jackets. The tall one with the short hair had extraordinary blue eyes, but that is probably irrelevant. We were given special shoes to wear, like cotton slippers, and the older women were giggling—it was like dressing up. Inside, it was a museum like any other. The rooms strangely impersonal, exhibits arranged in cabinets against the wall, special objects located towards the centre.

We crowded around the guide. He spoke in a quiet voice.

'Before we proceed, I must ask you to refrain from smoking. What you see here are his possessions, and you will not find a single, solitary ashtray. He was living proof, you might say, against the anthropological argument that tobacco is an instinct fundamental to man. Some people'—here, a note of disapproval altered his voice—'out of malice, or to test him, would give him expensive ashtrays as gifts. We have a small room full of them.'

'Goodness!'

'The other thing, of course, is that smoke has a corrosive effect on permanent exhibits. This is well known.'

'Like the cave-paintings in Lascaux, France.'

'Exactly. Now—'

'What about drink?' a man asked, interrupting.

'He took the occasional small glass, in private. Now'—turning to the first exhibit—'here we have his chair. This he sat on during his last twenty-five years, received visitors in it, and so on. Notice the flattened contour of the seat. Caused by his body-weight.'

The chair was immediately surrounded. Last year, the museum attracted 142,870 visitors from all corners—tourists, family people, and even businessmen. There were two New Zealanders down the front wearing nylon haversacks. They had the best positions.

The chair, a soft brown one, had ordinary curved sides, and a blurred stain where his head must have been. Although it was encased completely in glass they'd put a piece of rope across the arms as double protection, like a man who wears a belt as well as suspenders. It was easy to imagine him sitting there, hunched slightly forward, his body-weight exerting pressure downwards.

Someone asked, 'Was he such a heavy man?'

'I can tell you,' the guide replied. 'The pictures you've seen tend to suggest a large man. Last recorded his weight was actually 113 lbs. (51 kilos). He had an abhorrence of figures, by the way—as you probably know. Preferred pronouncements, slogans, instructions, counter-proposals, manifestos, modifications to previous judgements. That sort of thing.'

'I haven't seen any photographs,' said a number of people, fairly loudly.

The guide who had moved off waited patiently at the next exhibit. South Americans and others were quickly taking photos of the empty chair. They rejoined wearing that peculiar breathless expression of photographers, as our guide was reminiscing.

'I remember the day we met. He was speaking and looking at me. I listened. It was as though guns were thundering . . . he had that effect. My experience of his magnetism, but purely personal. Then he died at seventy, almost seventy-one. I remember the day as if it were yesterday.'

An austere Englishman murmured, 'Three score and ten . . .'

'To some of us,' the guide went on, 'it seemed impossible that he would die. His sheer presence was something . . .'

His voice (or his memory) trailed off.

Everyone waited, then followed his hand as it tapped the top of the cabinet.

Horizontal, neatly labelled, was a piece of blue carpet, raised to waist level where it could be studied closely.

'This was taken from under his desk,' the guide explained. 'He had the habit of clearing his throat, and at the same time shuffling his feet. Those worn patches you see were made by his shoes—size eights. In effect he has *scratched evidence of his existence on earth*, materially speaking, although to us onlookers now, we can conjure up all kinds of thoughts. What was he thinking as his feet shifted and scraped? Was he frowning?'

Having asked these questions the guide himself peered at the carpet.

'We were anxious to include one of his shoes, but could only obtain the sock you see on the left. Black. For all his boldness he was basically conservative.'

Our surprise must have shown, for he smiled.

'Conservative, yes, in dress.'

The worn carpet was strangely compelling. Then the sock. It was dirty and needed mending.

We moved on to another room, following the guides. With each step we seemed to draw closer to him, acquiring greater knowledge, like a fan spreading outwards.

And there in the next room stood a tall empty rectangle, of wood, painted cream. It too was roped off so nobody could 'use' it.

'Gallows?' a man said, aloud.

In every pack there's a joker. This one was middle-aged with a rectangular face, holding a girlfriend in her twenties. She was the one who laughed.

The guide cleared his throat.

'This is important. If you could look at this. His *body* travelled through what you see before you, sometimes several times a day. If he paused in this doorway, as I'm sure he did, his shape would have been framed; and since no full-length portrait exists this is the nearest we have. All that is required,' he said, staring at the joker, 'is a little imagination.'

He stepped back and the doorway was quickly surrounded. Women put on the expression they use when choosing wallpaper. One of them touched the guide's sleeve. 'The photographs. Where can we see his photograph?'

'Ah, the postcard counter had some, but I think they've sold out.'

'Oh, that's too bad.'

'They've all sold out?'

Then the Englishman spoke up. Like several others, he was taking notes.

'How tall was he?'

The guide knew exactly.

'Neatly palindromic! 1.81 metres. If you prefer it, 5 foot 10. He had—let's see—a foot to spare in the doorway. Nevertheless, he instinctively stooped. This gave the impression, to some, that he was a man of *humility.*'

Everyone laughed. How could anyone think such a thing?

Smiling, the guide said, 'Let me ask you a question. Is humour more important than history?'

Now obviously this was directed at the joker. A murmur spread as the question was repeated. The Englishman tapped his nose with a silver propelling pencil. Humour more important than history? One of the young ones, a student wearing sandshoes, replied by asking a question:

'Did he laugh? Was he that sort of type?'

'Yes,' a woman added; she had hairs above her lip. 'Was he *happy?*'

The student turned to her.

'You're confusing the issue. I said, Did he laugh—not whether he was happy or not.'

'I'm sorry! I don't see the difference.'

She turned to the rest of us. I thought she was going to cry.

The guide smiled at the floor.

'Happiness,' he said, 'is notoriously difficult to describe.'

People began nodding.

'The most rudimentary textbook tells us it takes seventeen facial muscles to laugh, yet only three to frown. So! His most obvious quality was not so much happiness *per se*, but the ability to attract loyalty. People looked up to him. He became an inspiration...a comparison. Would that occur if he was patently happy? I think that is the question we should be asking.'

Mmmmm.

Lips were pursed. Most, I think, took the point. No one added to it; and the guide moved silently away to the side wall.

A woman whispered to her husband, 'Arnold, my legs are sore.'

'Not yet. Listen to what the man is saying.'

The guide was pointing at marks on the wall.

'A similar exhibit to the doorway. He came here one morning and happened to sit down. We think he was trying to remember something. Anyway, it was right here. And this is the shape his shadow made.'

The lines on the wall suddenly made sense, like a country on a map, unvisited, but quite familiar. Helpful arrows pointed to features which might otherwise have gone unnoticed: NOSE FROM SIDE, CHIN (WHILE NOT SPEAKING), ELBOW, SITE OF HANDS, PELVIS, etc.

'Apart from knowing that he sat right *here*,' said the guide quietly, 'it does provide some idea of his body *mass*, although what you see is one-dimensional. He grew from something small into this shape. All the graduations, his history of growth, are contained therein, but invisible. It doesn't quite show his thinness, but the stoop of his shoulders is evident.'

So we were standing a yard or two from where he had sat! It produced powerful sensations: curiosity, silence. Then people could be heard trying to work out the position of the limbs, filling in the outline.

A woman complained, 'Well, I like to know the colour of a man's eyes.'

'Grey,' someone told her.

'Weren't they blue? I thought I saw a picture once.'

While they argued others went on with the guide, trailing as you do in museums, searching ahead for things not yet seen.

We entered a small room which had a simple coffee table, glass-topped, placed in the centre. The guides exchanged smiles as we crowded around, trying to work this one out. A coffee table. Was that all? The student noticed a little arrow on the glass. It encouraged discussion, speculation. The young man was quite eager now: 'I think I see something else too.'

Then the guide stepped in.

'Very good. We almost missed this one ourselves. I am referring, of course, to the fingernail trapped under the glass. He must have been trimming, and it snicked out, to lodge down between the sides.'

A woman pulled a face.

'Is that worth preserving?'

'It's part of him,' the guide reminded her.

Clearly, some of the womenfolk thought it pointless.

'A small example,' the guide argued, 'of the growth of his extremities.'

If only the fingernail was easier to see; I think perhaps that was the trouble. It could then be examined closely and carefully. A raised platform and special lighting would do the trick.

'So much is unknown about great men,' said the guide, moving towards a showcase opposite, 'that every scrap of evidence plays its part . . . piecing together the whole.'

Here, he showed us a cup and plate, still dirty, mounted on velvet.

The joker elbowed his girlfriend: 'The Last Supper.'

The guide didn't seem to hear.

'Undoubtedly, the plate is the most important. Traces of his last meal are visible: lamb chops, mashed potatoes, carrot with peas. On the edge there you can see traces of ketchup.'

Too many people were trying to see. Flashlights began sparking. Those New Zealanders had the best positions again. There was some ill-natured shoving.

'Some of you come around near me,' the guide demanded, before continuing. The other guides pushed the timid ones inwards.

'You perhaps know about his appetite. It was so healthy it made certain people upset. Somehow they assumed all famous men would have perfect table manners! But he sat down to eat, nothing else, and to get it over with as soon as possible.'

'I had no idea!' declared a lady; and she spoke for others.

'Surely,' said the New Zealanders, both turning, 'it's a sign of honesty.'

The joker laughed.

The guides nodded however.

'If ever a man deserved food it was he. Who was it said: we must eat in order to think?'

'I know!' shouted the student. Heads turned in his direction. He pulled faces and went on clicking his fingers.

'God, now I've forgotten . . .'

The cup and plate put us in a subdued, reflective mood. It forced us to see him from an ordinary, unexpected angle: bent, inserting food into his mouth. Quite opposite to the established picture. Yet, instead of reducing our interest it seemed to bring him closer.

A few yards away a much smaller cabinet.

'I think this one can be passed over quickly,' the guide said, scratching his neck. 'We are still in the throes of deciphering it. One of his habits was to slip out unnoticed and mingle with ordinary people. He liked to keep in touch. This is a bus ticket he used one afternoon. One of us found it, still crumpled. You will appreciate that to keep it in its original state—screwed into a ball by one of his hands—means the number cannot be read. His destination on that day remains unknown. But that's our problem. And we're working on it. Now, if you could step along here . . .'

The woman with aching legs held him by the sleeve. He turned, frowning. 'Bob, show this lady to the toilets.'

The rest including her husband went on; but two or three, led by the young man, crawled underneath the cabinet, squinting up at the bus ticket, perhaps hoping for the edge of a number, or something not noticed by the museum staff. They returned dusting themselves, wearing thoughtful expressions.

By then our group found itself divided by a strange barricade. It jutted out from a wall, V-shaped. Thus it ingeniously prevented each onlooker 'using' the exhibit—a mirror fixed fairly high on the wall. Naturally people tried. A woman (with rubbery lips) had one hand poised for automatic hair-adjustment; and unable to stop the process took out a hand mirror.

Our guide waited for quiet. I noticed he perspired slightly.

'His mirror: its importance must be apparent to everyone. For at least twelve years'—he paused to let it sink in—'it registered his image several times a day. What is perhaps important: it has been established he was the last person to use it. His face, which was drawing to a close, was the last to be registered. And,' he added, bowing his head, 'we intend to keep it that way.'

Nobody spoke.

An old member of the group, but wearing a floral shirt, said, 'He used it for shaving, for instance.'

The guide nodded.

'Odd thing was, you all know what he looks like—the bushy hair sticking out—[I think he said bushy hair sticking out]—well, he found as he grew older he had to shave *more*. I say odd, because that's against the physiological trend.'

The floral shirt nodded.

'I only use the razor every two days now.' He turned to us. 'It's not a nice feeling, I can tell you.'

'Three score and ten,' murmured the Englishman again.

'Oh, don't let's bring any gloom into this.'

Feet shuffled. We were strangers, but a vague unpleasantness spread.

'His shaving gear is in that cabinet there. But for some reason it doesn't attract as much interest as other exhibits.'

So we missed that one and, after seeing his pillow and a photograph of the sky taken from his window, assembled around what looked like a stamp-dealer's cabinet. Out of the corner of my eye I noticed the guides shepherding back a middle-aged couple; they must have wandered off.

Ours gave a sudden smile.

'Who here takes an interest in graphology?'

A man, who hadn't spoken before, shrugged, 'We all do. It's extremely difficult to avoid.'

The guide laughed. He was one of those men who say '*touché*'.

Four specimens of handwriting were laid out in rows: character was bound to be revealed. The pushing and shoving increased as everybody tried to see, some using their elbows; but the lucky ones down the front suddenly lifted their heads.

'This is no damned good. It's nothing.'

I think many of us felt disappointed then.

'It's upside down.'

'Yes, yes,' conceded our guide, 'these sheets were taken from his desk. He had one of those blotters with leather corners.'

'What's the point then?'

'It's one stage removed,' admitted our guide. 'But! Why should you expect everything to be so clearly revealed? Let us admit it: he was not easy to understand. We were with him! We know! He could be quite nasty sometimes. Vain. Often moody. Some days childish almost. But a genius. A man of his calibre cannot be "read" head-on. As it is, you are privileged to be standing as close as you are now.'

'But—'

'Excuse me, the blotter denotes his former presence, the weight of his body. His elbow must have rested on the edges.

He used a blotter because he was born in the nineteen-tens. His thoughts were "dried" by the blotter. So far as his actual hand is concerned it was small with long descendencies. The signature was rapid though, with appropriate flourishes.' He smiled again. People were nodding. 'After signing a letter he'd sit back and say, "There now!" '

'I wrote to him once,' said a man sadly. 'He never answered.'

'Ah, there were many demands on his time. And you could have been a crackpot. All sorts wrote to him with strange requests, heart-rending ones even. You can imagine. He had to be ruthless.'

And so people looked again; and it wasn't long before they were pointing and exclaiming, identifying the occasional word. The guide finally had to clap his hands, and quite loudly a second time, although not in an annoyed way, before anyone moved; and then a man and his wife remained, intent on reading the 'handwriting'.

We saw a smooth piece of yellow soap (thought to be his), tweezers for removing unwanted hairs, and the old belt that held up his trousers for thirteen years. We saw his shirt size (15), hot-water bottle, the tennis shade he used when reading. Some of us were tired. Naturally. How far had we walked? Then across a room we saw a wall covered in what appeared to be advertisement posters.

These were tradesmen's calendars, twenty or thirty years arranged chronologically, the days crossed off with various pens and pencils, a pretty quilted effect. It illustrated the span of his life, the abruptness of death.

Words were unnecessary.

Several made sad, clicking sounds with their tongues.

'He must have had,' said someone admiringly, 'a strictly methodical mind to mark his days like that. I'm surprised.'

This brought a simple answer.

'It's out of fashion these days,' a man said. 'People tend to use mechanical self-advancing calendars.'

The group nodded. There was wisdom in that.

Then I think it was the Englishman who spoke.

'One knows he was methodical, even fastidious. There are those stories too about his tightness with money. It's all connected. But what was he really like? One only knows *about* him.'

At this the guide became angry.

'You say he was fastidious. All right. But I would have thought the way to study a man is not by trivia and gossip, but by his influence. This museum—created with some difficulty, I might add—concentrates on showing the *force* of his existence. He had weaknesses, of course. Great men are invariably selfish, intolerant. He disliked drunks, advertising, talk of the weather, women's perfumes, cigarette ash, indecision, coat-hangers, and fools.'

He waited as some of us found scraps of paper, the backs of envelopes, to take this down.

'He was uncomfortable with the opposite sex. He disliked oranges, and anyone touching him. Never married. Towards the end of his life he'd smile at the heads of small children. His pyjamas were striped flannel. He was always hungry, although he never exceeded 113 lbs. He was suspicious of photography, but later grew to respect it. Any questions? No. Then we'll carry on.'

But there was a general reluctance to move, so absorbed were we in the list he'd given us, adding it to what we already knew. A clearer picture was beginning to emerge, and with it a kind of spreading elation. We felt we were standing close to him, on the very edge of important, intimate knowledge. To move would break the flow. The guides however began clapping and pushing, whistling like drovers, and so we became confused. One of our number shouted, 'Quit this shoving. We're moving, we're moving.'

So we entered, or were herded into, the adjoining room, probably the last, for we could hear the turnstiles clicking behind a wall. Our bad temper could have been due to museum-fatigue. It had taken a steady toll. Some stood one-legged like African birds, linoleum tiles on concrete not exactly helping.

The guide was all smiles. He must have noticed our annoyance. He pointed to the now-typical glass cabinet.

Almost immediately those in front drew back, the women especially; they could not disguise their disgust. All I could see was a shallow metal tray.

The guide cleared his throat. 'Not everyone's cup of tea, this one. I should explain: we were in two minds whether to include it or not. But to be squeamish would be to miss the point. Bodily functions are at once both fundamental and intensely personal. Remember too the banal fact that nothing succeeds in levelling a man than the sight, or the concept of, his ordure.'

'You mean "shit," ' said a figure down the front, one of the New Zealanders. Turning to us, he grinned. 'There's a turd on the tray here.'

'Dejecta. Coprological data,' corrected the guide.

I wondered how they'd got it.

The joker put his handkerchief up to his nose.

'*Please*,' said a woman with a pained expression. 'You're not funny.'

The guide quickly went on, 'Interesting to realise the obvious: that this was inside him, and rejected by him. Let me say that again. This was *part* of him, part of—for want of a better word—his life-force. Hence its undoubted importance.'

Hearing this, people returned to the cabinet, and some began making rapid sketches. This encouraged others. A flash-bulb went off. Those towards the back soon found it difficult to glimpse a corner of the tray, let alone appraise the substance inside. The fascination may well have been primordial. That would explain the persistent but blank expressions people assumed as they pushed forward, anxious to improve their positions. Again, noticeably less interested were the womenfolk. One had elbowed her way out, saying, 'The last thing I want to see is that.'

She was ignored.

The guides stood together, hands in their pockets, surveying the scene. Ten or fifteen minutes passed before our man spoke up.

'Please,' he said in a loud voice. 'This way, please. Thank you. One final item is here.' Adding, over his shoulder, 'A recent, major acquisition.'

This is the small room by the exit door. A cabinet was lit by a single spotlight. Under glass lay the handpiece (only) of a black telephone. Attached was a foot or so of dusty cord: ripped from a wall.

'And through these wires,' the guide was saying, 'through

the electrical copper, springs, the black *bakelite* you see, he spoke, propelled his thoughts.'

The two guides were looking over our shoulders. They were breathing reverently.

We could see dandruff caked on the earpiece.

'His breath travelled along these wires, his personality travelled along these wires.'

The words fell on the discarded telephone. The rest of the room lay in darkness. Someone coughed. 'Any questions?' asked the guide.

Then a woman asked, 'What was his voice like?'

I think that was one of the things we all wanted to know.

The guide, clearing his throat, smiled. 'Let me attempt an imitation.'

Paradise

Breaking into light, this long silver bus. It comes rumbling from its concrete pen. Grunting away. It reaches North Terrace by stopping and yawning; its full length swings.

Yawns left, climbs past Rosella, hesitates at Maid 'n Magpie, take the left, roads are empty, petrol stations are empty, car yards are empty, shops are empty, hold her steady, chassis doesn't pitch then, there are couples behind curtains, there's a dog, watch him, man on a bike, shiftworker in a coat probably. Now the road's stirring, milkman turns a corner, leaves the road open, driver taps the steering-wheel, enormous view of life in the morning, foot taps contented by it.

The bus had PARADISE printed on the front, sides and back. It was a long run to the suburb. At the outer reaches it specialised in young married women with prams; and Merv Hector had to smile. From his position in the driving seat he could see the new-generation hairdos, skirts, worried eyebrows. Gentle, slow-eyed Hector waited for them, was happy to be of service. When one of them waved between stops he would open the doors every time. His conductors were quick to see they were riding with a soft heart. Straightforward characters, they were quick to assert themselves. 'Be an angel, Merv. Stop at the shops there for some smokes.' They also went to him when sick of things.

This time his conductor was Ron. His voice, tightly pitched. 'Getting up at this hour really makes me wonder. We're not carrying a soul. Look, it really makes me sick.'

Merv shook his head. Through the pure windscreen the road was alive ahead of him. Below his feet the bus was really travelling. It made you feel alive.

'There's the people we get on the way back,' Merv said.

He made a long sentence of it, as he did when contented, and he heard Ron's breath come out dissatisfied.

'There's too bloody many then. We should have two here serving then. All the schoolkids; they never have to pay properly. What time is it?'

They were entering Paradise. As usual Hector waited to be thrilled by it, he stared and was ready, but a disappointment spread like the morning shadows. Streets were golden but it seemed more like a finishing sunset than the beginning of a day. When he stopped the bus it seemed to be further away— Paradise did. New tiles pointing in the sky spoilt the purity. But Paradise could be close by. It felt close by. The air light, bright; he was at the edge of something. Hector's stubborn fifty-four-year-old eyesight produced these messages for his heart but he was required to turn the bus, and he turned the bus around.

'Hell, we're going to really get hot and crowded.'

It was Ron running his finger around his collar.

'She'll be right,' said Hector.

'Hang on a sec. Let us out at the shop. You want some chewy?'

Stopped. Merv Hector was mild cheese from Norwood. At the MTT he was considered slow and forgetful. But he was dependable enough, and voiced no objections to the long early morning runs. His moon wife was stupefied by his sincerity. He was older. Their garden grew weeds. His watch was inaccurate, and he stumbled near the garden. 'Dear?' he sometimes said to Enid and faded out. The distance to Paradise, with the great screen framing all kinds of life, gave him this gentle advice: move, slow down, stop, let them get on, move, see, Paradise. The world was beautiful. It was plainly visible.

Now Ron said something again.

'Look at all those bloody kids. Just what I need. All right! Move down the back!'

The bus grew squatter and fatter with the weight of everybody. Ron battled through, and the air was hot and human. They were now channelled by houses near the city, yet it was confusing.

A green bread van turned while Merv wondered. The shape was smacked by the metal at Merv's feet and the whole green turned over and over like a dying insect, a round pole came zooming forward, Hector's world entered it and splintered. Glass splattered. A crying uniform over Hector's shoulder cracked the windscreen.

There was the crash, Hector remembered. And the memory of Paradise persisted. If there was a beautiful place he could watch for like that.

He was wrinkling and gave a twitch.

He found other work.

'Morning.'

'Morning. Six, thanks.'

'Six, and?'

'Eight.'

'Right there.'

'Two for me.'

'Back a bit, sir. Up we go.'

Inside a driver's uniform again. They hold their breaths and stare at lights blinking: 4, 5, feel the altitude moving below the toes, 6, blink, blink, 7, 8, turn the lever, doors further up: whrrp! Abrupt stop, men breathe into ears, business-face veins, Windsor knots left-right-centre. Right this little lift will help, reach the top, an essential task in the latest glass architecture.

I'll go to heaven.

Merv Hector settled on his stool in the lift. Shuffling and throat-clearing squashed the space into a noise box. Like the run to Paradise, he was at the entrance with a mild face, helping them: they stepped out at certain vertical intervals, sped down horizontal tunnels for special meetings. These repetitions gave him the most gentle pleasure. He was in the centre of activity and happily assisting. His placid role in giving this regular service, regular service, settled his features.

In the mornings a lemon-headed man unlocked the building and the lifts.

'How are you today?'

'What are you this early for?' the caretaker answered.

'Well,' Hector began.

The caretaker cut him off. 'If the others come here late, you've got to get here at this hour.'

'It's a good building you've got,' Hector suggested, in all seriousness.

'What's good about it? You don't have to live in it.'

And Hector had to take some keys to him one morning right up to the eighteenth floor. He was touched by the high silence. Outside, the wind scratched at the glass. Inside, currents of cold air tugged at his sleeve like the mysterious breathing of a giant snowman. It was some height, near the clouds. God. Hector marvelled. His veins, his eyes seemed to be swelling. Was this pleasure? It must be nearer to heaven, or Paradise up there.

'What's your trouble?'

The caretaker came up behind.

'Give us the keys, and scoot. They're buzzing you.'

Merv ran back to the lift.

'Is it all right if I bring my lunch on the roof?' he called out.

'Christ Almighty!' the caretaker said.

Why, the roof was high. It was peaceful. He could watch noises made by the street people below. And clouds closed in; could almost touch him. And someone had placed pot plants along the edge, and wind trembled their green. Did the lonely caretaker put them there? The slow question gently surrounded him with pleasure, and near the clouds he chewed on Enid's sandwiches.

The lift was always crowded. He kept going up down, up down, all day. Now he preferred going up to down. Going down it was back to the street, hot and old. So he kept going up, and late one morning kept going, kept going, and, wondering, crashed into the ceiling. Roof hit roof—or there where springs to stop him. But it was enough to jump him off the stool, and the caretaker arrived.

'No one's ever done that before, you bloody fool.'

'Strike,' said Hector.

He was dazed.

Merv Hector continued. His hour on the roof was something to look forward to. I'm very near it, he said in the silence. Full of pretty, dazed visions he slept past two, and was immediately fired by the caretaker.

'Even if you come here early,' said the caretaker, signalling up and down with his arm. 'Useless, useless.'

Hair on Hector's head looked electrocuted. It was fifty-four-year-old stuff flaking and greying: always looked as he had left a speedboat. He wore brown eyeglasses. Sometimes he touched his lips with his fingers vibrating, exactly as though they played a mouth organ.

Home with Enid she carried on a bit.

But she noticed something. He had been weeding the garden. One finger was cut by a buried piece of china—a broken prewar saucer of some description—and self-pity moved him to silence. He seemed to dry up. More or less alone, he shaved vaguely. He didn't say much.

He was not his cheery self, she said.

'Why don't you get another job, dear? We can settle down after.'

Hector agreed.

'You sit there,' the young man pointed. 'The phone goes, write down what they say. Just sit here. The bureau rings about every half hour. Arrange the switches like so. You can make any words they tell you. At the moment it's RAIN DEVELOPING.'

Hector looked through the tiny window, looked across the wall of the building and there, in enormous lights, were the words RAIN DEVELOPING.

'If we had an automatic system,' the young man said, 'you wouldn't have to mess around with all these switches. But it's easy enough.'

'Yes,' admitted Hector absently.

So this is how the weather lights work, he thought.

This is what I do.

The room was tiny, concrete: enough to depress anybody. It was high in the dead part of the building, ignored by the air-conditioning. A plastic ashtray sat on the small table.

The black phone gave a sudden ring. A voice told him to change the message to RAIN. 'Right, then,' said Hector. He fiddled with switches, concentrating, then turned them on. Through the window he saw the sudden change in the message and automatically wondered what the people below thought. Would they believe in that? Would they notice his sign? How many would be caught without coats, umbrellas, rudimentary shelter?

But there was no rain—not a drop. Standing at the window he became concerned. Merv looked at his message. He looked down at the people shapes moving casually. Then, miraculously it seemed, rain began hitting and splashing. His sign shined in triumph; and the thought that his warning had saved people flooded him with a specific pleasure. It was good, and he clenched himself. He looked up then at the clouds. They seemed to be pressing down on his room, around his life, down his mouth, showering his vision with rain. God, he wondered.

Down on the street depressed figures ran from point to point. The shining traffic remained queued, steam rose, and three silver buses waited bumper to bumper. It recalled certain mornings behind the steering wheel, the giant screen wipers scanned repetitiously like radar, squish-a-squish. Now he stared through the glass window, up at the clouds, up into the heart of the rain. He felt settled, sure, safe, glad to be there; he thought of home, the maroon chair, and his Enid.

Nothing's the matter, he said. I'm fine, he wanted everyone to know. On the panel he moved across and switched the message to FINE.

The huge bright lights said FINE as the rain kept splashing down. Altogether, Merv Hector marvelled at every single thing. He stared at his sign. It was true. He loved the clouds. It was another world, and he was there. The phone began to ring.

Ore

The list of publications Wes Williams read carefully, especially between the lines.

Petroleum Intelligence Weekly
Wolfrom's Commodity Digest
Financial Review
London Financial Times (Sat. only)
Sugar Review
Tin International
Skinner's Mining International Yearbook
Rydge's
Pamphlets from chartists. Annual reports.
Statements from as far away as Detroit—when America catches a cold the rest of the world gets pneumonia. Sundry newspapers.

• • •

In the saloon bar, legs apart, he spoke with a kind of mechanical earnestness, looking over the heads of the others. He and his friends wore the short-sleeved shirt; with a tie of course. They could have been tennis players showered and combed after a match. In fact they were from the one office. Wes has pale eyes like the water in one of those Sydney swimming pools, a small mouth and large wrist knuckles. About thirty odd.

They were talking about the gold price.

'It was a cert. It was on the cards. The Americans had to let it go,' Wes said simply.

Each was familiar with the other's arguments, predictions, yet never tired of hearing them. 'Shares' were an infectious, endlessly comforting disease. It affected the nasal passages. If someone changed the subject, even to cars, Wes would look around, restless, till it returned.

Wes had a few sugar shares—bought on the crest of the nickel boom. Everybody knew that. But Wes had recently moved into gold as well. He was keeping quiet about that, though anyone could tell, if they opened their eyes, he had assumed the complacent, almost deaf, manner of an 'insider'.

'Tell you what, copper'll go next.'

Ha, ha. Wes was always on about copper.

'The currency crisis,' Wes went on. 'It'll affect the commodities. Copper's fucking low anyway.'

'The Cobar mine's doing all right.'

Wes smacked his lips.

'Give me Mt Isa any day.'

Gazing over their heads he threw in a tonnage and price-earnings ratio. Then bulging his stomach, pressing his chin to his chest, he gave two short belches: something he always did after the first few mouthfuls of beer. It was a free country.

The trouble was, the others could only go on about iron ore. The finer arguments on gold, copper, and silver, their relationships to the dollar and so forth, were beyond them. Really, completely.

Wes Williams first became aware he was different shortly after he had his teeth filled. Since buying his sugar shares he'd chewed sweets whenever he could and put too much sugar in people's tea, including his own; and one day actually leaned on his secretary's morning cake, destroying it 'accidentally': all in his own way to help raise, or at least hold, the world sugar price. He had only—what—forty-one ordinary shares, but it was the largest sugar company in the Southern Hemisphere. The distant logic that 'every grain must count' had spread throughout his mind to his arms and eyes, the way sugar itself is altered by moisture. He thought of the sugar that went into wedding cakes, and enjoyed all marriages. Empty trays in delicatessen windows caught his eye. Chewing gum in a gutter was another good sign. These things can really add up. A really pleasant dream, one he had replayed in broad daylight, was of a line of trucks leaving a refinery, each with a hole in the floor, the precious stuff running out like sand, or time, unknown to the driver, until the trucks arrived empty—although Williams was yet to hear of such a case. He took a keen interest in hurricanes if any were reported heading towards the Caribbean islands.

His dentist went busy and grim. Williams needed seven gold fillings.

The 1969–70 mining boom possessed its own mythology now. It was incredible. Poseidon had been written up in *Time* magazine. 'Great Boulder', 'Carr Boyd Rocks', 'Western Mining' were names similar in feeling to 'Burke and Wills', 'Leichhardt', 'Ayers Rock', their modern equivalents perhaps, although that wasn't why Wes preferred them to the industrials.

The following day the price of gold fixed at $US35 an ounce was allowed to float. The wealth in Williams' mouth doubled overnight.

Hectic scenes were photographed at the Sydney stock exchange—men shouting and waving papers. Some experts were talking about $130 an ounce. Meanwhile his friends stood around talking, and looking, small-time.

He could scarcely contain himself.

Up to $117 in no time.

Williams ran his tongue around his mouth. Main gold-producing countries: Russia, South Africa. If the blacks went mad now, destroyed a few mines . . .

Wes nodded carefully.

'It'll crack a hundred and fifty, no worries.'

The spread in holdings made him feel diversified, secured successfully. It seemed there were more things of interest in the world, more to occupy his mind. At home he had 'files' and a book where he kept track of his shares. Regularly he added up the dividends collected so far. Wes was a bit tight. Even Judith, his wife, could get irritated. But it wasn't a bad flat. At six you needed sunglasses in the lounge.

She had a part-time job somewhere, which helped.

No, you had to be on the lookout. Since the nickel boom

he'd missed—Christ—the land boom, the cocoa boom, and the rubber boom. So had his friends. And they were looking the other way when Persian carpets, then paintings by Australian artists, took off. Australiana books Wes knew nothing about; brass beds he'd heard were a good thing but already high; original bushranger posters few and far between. You never know. There was a chance of stumbling across a pair of real convict handcuffs one day. Abo axeheads. Where could you get hold of them now?

Literally, the world consisted of objects beckoning, about to leap in value.

'Mt Isa' seemed to be waving from the share lists, signalling before it was too late. That was what it was like: a name detached itself with its stark pithead, geologist's camp, future prospects . . .

On the 27th, a Friday, gold topped $148 an ounce.

Williams could think of nothing else. Much of his job at the office was done automatically, the attention he paid his wife became distracted noticeably. Food was tasteless.

Mt Isa also had silver, lead. A large slab of the capital was held by the US parent. See, these were factors that his friends never took into account.

Arriving home one night he told Judith about the market, as matter-of-factly as possible. He even sketched out the gold tier-system for her. She was painting her toenails. 'Isn't "bamboo" the most beautiful word in the world?' she asked, not looking up. He noticed then she was naked.

'What are you doing like this?' he shouted.

She wasn't listening.

'What's this you're reading?'

He picked up *Lasseter's Last Ride*.

'Ion Idriess?'

'Give it back, please.'

He was about to, and would have chucked it; but he couldn't put it down.

Wes sat up with a headache and the taste of old pennies in his mouth. This was funny. He'd never felt crook in his life before.

'You were talking in your sleep,' his wife complained.

'Nothing dirty, I hope.'

This bloody headache!

'Something about Mary Kathleen,' said Judith in a flat voice.

Perhaps no man can absorb as many numerical figures as Williams did at that time. While Judith was talking he studied his teeth in the bathroom and farted. That was better. He carried the world's copper reserves around in his head, and much valuable supporting data, including core samples and lode depths, 'promising situations'. Ordinary news failed to register. There was no room. Occasionally, he squeezed in a political movement from Zambia or Chile; but that was tied up with copper. Optical wonders such as an iron ball swinging through one of the city's old buildings passed without his mouth opening.

The headache came in waves. Stranger was the taste of pennies. It reminded him of the ore piled up outside Mt Isa; but then so did mould on his cheese at lunch one day. His head continued its slow cracking.

No need to tell his wife.

He found a doctor. Here was an eminent specialist, an expert in his field. He had a paisley handkerchief almost falling out from his lapel pocket. He wore tortoise-shell glasses.

As he shone a torch down Wes's mouth he constantly changed the shape of his own mouth.

'And you've been off appetite?'

Before Williams could nod a thermometer rose from his mouth. Mercury! Interesting, mysterious metal. How about mercury? Not traded enough though, not in the big league. Wes subsided. And he'd caught sight of the doctor's cuff links: solid gold.

'How long have you been out?' Wes asked, stretching his legs. 'I take it you're from the UK?'

Macquarie Street, thought Wes. He'd be doing all right.

The doctor took the thermometer to the window.

'It was actually a Friday morning, August, 1969.'

'Just in time,' Wes called out. 'Poseidon, Western Mining. I s'pose you got some shares?'

Everyone else did.

'You seem to have a fever,' the doctor said, shaking the thermometer. 'Yes, I did as a matter of fact.'

'Still goddem?'

Wes relaxed. One of the things about the mining boom was its spontaneous camaraderie.

'Still goddem?'

'I am afraid so.'

'Copper,' said Wes loudly, in case he was speaking here with a man disillusioned with the market. 'That's going to move.'

The doctor smiled.

'You think so?'

'Well, I'd buy now,' Wes advised him. 'Hang on. Whoow,' he said, suddenly sitting down. 'I'm as dizzy as buggery. Fuck this!'

Copper broke through the psychological £500 barrier at the London Metal Exchange; the Australian producers quickly followed. Big fall in warehouse stocks. The Zambian railway cut. China was reported buying.

The taste in Wes's mouth became so strong Judith must have noticed. On top of her he found he could hold off by picturing the layout of a famous open-cut mine. On the other hand, his head was so full of figures it rejected breakfast.

At the doctor's now he noticed the *Financial Review* alongside *Punch* and the *Autocar*.

Wes thought he could slap him on the back; because of the terrific mood just then.

'There you are, six hundred and fifty this morning. What did I tell you?'

It left sugar for dead.

The doctor gazed at him, tapping his teeth with a pencil.

'Several of my colleagues,' he said, 'have expressed an interest.'

Wes wasn't sure what he was getting at.

'We shall have to take a sample. A smallish operation. Your permission is required, of course.'

'Well, you're the experts,' said Williams loudly.

In case he was seriously ill or something he stumbled on.

'I'd say it was a moot point whether to buy a copper share now, or a ton of the metal itself.'

To his existing reserves Williams added discoveries of low-grade ore in Indonesia and Iran. Against that he put the latest consumption figures of the industrialised west; added acres of future cars and motorbikes, colour TV sets, fridges; eating into the known reserves. And what if Red China's economy took off? He rubbed his hands.

On the day, the doctor was unusually jovial yet didn't introduce him: nodded at Wes to lie down.

The others were 'specialists'. Each had the *Financial Review* under his arm. One wore a cork helmet. Another a handlebar moustache and cigar, though it was not yet ten o'clock in the morning. The third carried a superb English walking stick—worth a lot of money—but it was actually a theodolite. He was red in the face but grinning.

'Hello, old boy.'

'Pip, pip.'

'What?'

'I say.'

They crowded around.

'Standing at $2.70, with a yield of 6.3,' Wes began. He was a bit annoyed. They were now all calling him 'Mr Williams'. All part of their act.

They ignored his toneless predictions; lowered the bright lights, and murmured to each other. Some had their sleeves rolled up.

The first exploratory drilling encountered grey matter, nothing else.

The telephone rang.

'788.'

'5.6.'

The third and the fourth holes struck ore of major density, just below the surface. Further intersections proved the reserves. Open-cut was feasible. They all agreed. They had the equipment. It became a rapid large-scale operation. Wes's babbling went quieter, the figures became smaller, even dubious, until he was silent.

'That will be all. Thank you. You might take these tablets if you feel anything.'

Wes felt vaguely grateful. The others had gone; where were the others?

'No headache now? Good. Thank you, then.'

The doctor turned his back and began writing. Wes searched around for the taste of copper in his mouth. It too had gone.

Macquarie Street outside was sharply defined and noisy. Another hot day. The bar was empty, but Wes thought he'd wait there for the lunch crowd. Nothing else he could do. He looked around. No worries though. He adjusted himself on the stool. Diamond drilling intersected ore of major density.

Cul-de-Sac (uncompleted)

'Nevertheless, you can get there and back in two minutes,' said the Chief, wiping his hands. He said it a shade carelessly. Normally he was good at giving directions. Biv looked at the drawing board. It was necessary to move the T square. Then it was possible to see the position of the alleged, so-called cul-de-sac. Pencil lines converged towards it and stopped. So it was on the other side of town. This was going to take more than two minutes.

'Don't be a pain in the arse, son. You'd better leave this minute. The engravers are waiting. I'll show you how to get there.'

There are three main characters, four or five hangers-on, and bystanders who try to help but are more of a hindrance. Terrific scenery from now on.

78

The actual bridge, or a reconstruction of it, where the phrase *All That's Water under the Bridge* originated, was close to the cul-de-sac. Biv leaned over the parapet. Below ran an industrial conveyor belt; a 'mechanical' river. Flowing past were broken promises, yesterday's newspapers, wine bottles, telephone messages, clear insults, broken vases and expired insurance policies. A few pedestrians were leaning over trying to retrieve some of these objects. But their fingertips could only caress the slow-moving items spaced at irregular intervals on the belt. A fur coat went past, an unwanted child, a pair of size 32 underpants. A woman stretching down wept. A solemn man (husband?) placed a restraining hand on her shoulder blade, looking grim.

79

Biv walking to the horizon. Stone buildings and streets closed in behind, the way large leaves, elastic vines, apparently do in jungles. Ahead: supposed to be the cul-de-sac. He glanced at his watch, the strap held together by a rubber band (Biv is quite a character). In his hip pocket he carried the standard cartographer's compass. In the side pockets he'd fitted loaded rat traps in case of pickpockets. Just in case. Strapped to his left ankle was a pedometer, Made in Taiwan. Biv is the hero. He is walking smoothly, some would say striding, not far to go now. His Christian name, Roy. This is going to take more than two minutes.

80

There's Biv, his boss (often referred to here as 'Chief'), Grey next door, an optician with his eye on Biv, Grey's eldest daughter, several world-famous men, some shady characters who begin following Biv, though Biv's neighbour (Grey) doesn't come into the story at all.

81

All going according to plan. Ahead the suburb in question. Immediate left the tall aluminium building without a roof. This would be the new Trampolene Factory, well-known landmark. In front of which the new canal, in front of which the Helmet and Cap factory, in front of which the new Sand Museum, left of which . . .

Biv wrote in his notebook. 'Everything going according to plan. Our popular maps are perfectly true. The weather is holding up. I see the suburb in question ahead. Amen.'

82

But what are his weaknesses? What sort of 'character' is he? (What are Biv's 'characteristics'?) Is this to be a tragedy? After all, Biv is approaching thirty-six.

A note about his appearance.

He has blue hands; something to do with circulation. He has red ears; ditto. He has orange hair; the iron in his blood?

And like any topographer worth his salt he has worn elbows. When Biv bends his arm it is not a sharp angle, more a soft curve. He has measured the wear with set squares. However, don't have the idea Biv is a methodical character.

He is not a methodical character.

Also 'orange' is the deposit of wax in both ears. Yellowy is some mucus up his nose; green socks.

A bachelor.

83

He crouched between the brick wall and the palings. To see in, it was necessary to get himself caught in Grey's passionfruit vine. He had to wait quite a while. Then the light went on. Grey's eldest daughter moving around the dressing table slowly began undressing.

Those young though fully fledged shapes fell out of their restraining apparatus causing Biv's mouth to open. Some spittle ran down his chin. That always happens. She held her breasts in her hands and studied herself. Apparently satisfied she came over to the window, combing her hair, the sill slicing her at the knees, and faced Biv for a good thirty seconds: the blurred invitation between her legs like Tasmania. Biv, topographer, hopeful cartographer, thought of that afterwards.

84

Six or eight streets sloping down form an intersection, the streets like the legs of a spider. Biv was foolishly standing there working out the direction. Which street to take? He studied the compass. It was noon. Nobody around to ask the way. He heard a purring sound and something touched him. He turned. An empty pram had rolled down from one of the streets. Then he saw another coming to the left, then one straight ahead. Each one made a faint whirring sound. Prams attacked from all directions, from all the spider's legs. Some collided and overturned. No sooner did Biv jump aside than another would make him jump back, and then one he hadn't seen or heard cracked his shins. He fell. Prams surrounded him like animals. Prams banged into him. He shoved and kicked and ran swerving up one of the streets which proved to be empty. The optician watched him.

85

'A square is a reservoir; adjoining streets feed from it; streets and gutters are terrible parasites.' He entered the square; about time. The streets on all sides were lawn, the main traffic consisted of mowers crawling like insects. The square itself was bitumen. This composition, black bordered by green, was further enhanced by five dying pine trees forming a quincunx. A gardener was watering the one in the centre with a transparent can. Biv noticed it held several goldfish. Then he noticed the tree's shadow on the ground. It was *green*. He went over and lifted it. Naturally the shadow was cool, almost cold; and it was soft. There is nothing special about this, Biv should have told the gardener. Certain French artists employed green and even blue shadows back in the 1880s.

Instead, he asked the direction of the cul-de-sac.

'The feeling of space or the intuition of space is the most basic force of the mind,' the gardener replied.

I've heard that somewhere before, Biv thought to himself. 'This cul-de-sac. Where is it?'

He stamped his foot for added emphasis.

'Now look what you've done.'

The bitumen had cracked and four small rainbows seeped out. They held Biv's ankles. The gardener poured water over Biv's shoes. The rainbows subsided.

'I'm sorry.'

'The damage is done.'

'I'm sorry. I'll get a move on. I'll go on.'

86

The blue Staedtler 4B (considered to be the most beautiful pencil in the world) firm against the bevelled perspex drew the line north to the edge of . . . . the cul-de-sac.

Cul-de-sac?

Slid the set square along to the width (proportional) of an ordinary street. Halted. One inch equals half a mile. Sharpened the pencil. Resumed. Repeated parallel towards the cul-de-sac. His hand stood out purple and soft against the cartridge paper.

Road marked RD, or sometimes R.
Avenue AVE., space permitting.
Places of interest.
Museums and Art Galleries.
Parks and Police Stations.

87

Watching out of one eye while fitting a black horse with spectacles was the optician.

'I'm trying to trace a cul-de-sac,' Biv told him. He felt like talking to someone. His ankles and elbows were tired.

'What's that about you, Lazarus?'

Biv stepped back. The eye chart was so large the letters looked like a vertical highway. Only by stepping back half a mile, and keeping it in sight, bumping into pedestrians and lamp posts, could he read: CUL-DE-SAC. By then he was positioned very near to it. Truly this was a functional sign— a semaphore of the first order! Biv scribbled in his notebook. It was an innovation his Chief was bound to be interested in.

88

'The feeling of space or the intuition of space is the most basic force of the mind.'

'Rubbish. Absolute twaddle. Where have you been? Have I ever heard so much twaddle? Listen, my boy—'

89

Biv has a neighbour with ten fingers, two legs and three daughters, who doesn't come into this story. Grey is his name. Born at two in the morning, 1934. Grey has that passionfruit (growing wild). His hobbies, however, are holding colour transparencies up to the light and running model trains. He hasn't spoken to Biv for several years. His daughters whisper and laugh whenever Roy walks past. They can make his ears redden and pound from a distance of thirty yards. Crouching at night he watches the eldest undressing. One night there she noticed him watching.

90

'If truth is measurable, the work we do here is untainted. Our lines never lie. They trace concrete facts. Geometry—and topography is a branch of geometry—follows the behaviour of real objects. Always remember that. Your pencil is outlining reality. Where a line stops there's an intersection.'

'Everything should have a name,' Biv put in.

'Not while I'm talking. Listen to an older man. Then you might learn something. This job of ours is one of the few harmless professions left in the world. Stand up straight. Be proud of yourself.'

A strong point is Biv's way of listening, giving the odd nod, even to his Chief who is inclined to ramble just a bit.

'Besides,' the Chief was saying, 'consider the perfection of the straight line. Undeniable. And if the common right angle has a certain purity so too does the square. Besides,' he added, murmuring the obvious, 'the square is the only major shape that is man-made.'

91

On all fours inspectors holding large set squares check the angles of intersections, keeping the district 'straight'. There had been a vocal move from certain quarters, and letters to the newspapers, to increase the right angle from 90°. But here were the inspectors. They wore white coats and were accorded respect by the pedestrians. Often you would come across one on his knees. It made them look diseased. Speaking of calluses, Biv has one on the side of one finger where hundred of pencils have pressed over the years.

The residue of images. Shape and feel of precision instruments embed themselves in the mind.

Things he wanted to say; things he never said.

The things he never said to the Chief.

92

'There is a beauty in machinery and pipes. Wouldn't you agree?'

It was the optician standing beside him. He was wearing glasses with a false nose. 'Of course, some people don't agree,' he went on, admiring the view. 'They get their kicks out of natural spectacles. Personally, I think nature is over-rated. For one thing it is too dirty to be revered automatically. Look at the way mud isn't clean. And every other day I see dirty clouds in the shape of pudenda or testicles, et cetera.'

Biv hadn't looked at it that way before. Further spectacles unfolded before him.

A yard away crankshafts and pistons traced ephemeral crescents. Steam here was as beautiful as trees. Tubing and conduits! The various rivets! Hypnotic coils! Gauges flickered like the fingers of expensive women. All the metal hidden therein. Mild steel mainly, but a good deal of cast iron. Copper for proven qualities of insulation; copper conduits. Rubber though not a metal must be there, if hidden from view. Silver linings. Titanium in the paint. Magnesium in pistons — 35 per cent lighter and two and a half times stronger than aluminium. Molybdenum? And the sides of all nuts were tightened to face the same angle.

The optician removed his glasses and began weeping. 'Christ, it's beautiful,' he said. He stumbled over to a chrome-plated bucket close to the machinery. It was there to collect onlookers' tears.

'This machinery,' he explained, 'drives the city's fountains. Our fountains run on tears, but happy moisture not sadness.'

Biv also felt moved. Really, exhilarated. Then he glanced at his watch.

93

'Sit down,' his Chief told him. 'What do you eat for lunch?'
    'A pie.'

'A pie every twenty-four hours?'

Biv nodded.

The Chief scribbled figures beside the T square. Biv watched his neck, fascinated. Like the others his boss had patches sewn on his elbows and cuffs.

'Last year,' he declared, sitting back, 'you ate 198 pies. I estimate each weighs three-quarters of a pound. You've eaten over a hundredweight of pies, you greedy pig. I'm telling you this, Biv, for your own good. Quantities have a way of creeping up on us. Quantities affect a man's stamina.'

Biv was tired. He could feel it already.

94

Eminent citizens served time as statues. Granite plinths were distributed in prominent sites for this purpose. Geniuses, manufacturers, soldiers, encyclopaedists, the occasional explorer, climbed into position, usually in time for the morning rush hour. One would have thought that to be looked up to, to 'stand as an example', would be considered an honour, and although there was no shortage of candidates most put on bored, even bad-tempered expressions as they climbed into position. The job was tiring, especially for the older ones, under a blazing sun in summer, soaked to the marrow in winter, and they were busy men, still quite active in mind and body. Furthermore, an outstretched arm attracts pigeons. It was not uncommon to see a great poet step down, his head, shoulders and one arm covered in pigeon droppings. Perhaps for this reason the two-hour stint, or 'roster', had been devised.

They were not all geniuses though. Recently the list had been broadened, and the figures made to be more functional. It was agreed that writers while standing should also point to the library. Then a coalminer who had a savings account out of all proportion to his miserable earnings was allowed to stand and point to the bank. A woman who kept a spotless house balanced a vacuum cleaner on her head for the two hours. A celebrated meteorologist pointed up at the sky, though there was immediate confusion when a religious thinker insisted on doing the same. Athletes and weightlifters in flimsy shorts aimed a warning finger at the old people's home.

A person could go up and talk to these eminent figures. If you were lucky they would hand down valuable 'guidelines', or advice, based more often than not on a lifetime's experience.

Biv spoke to a middle-aged man who leaned forward slightly, one hand shading his eyes, squinting at the horizon.

'May I ask, what are your achievements?'

'Oh, I discovered some of the laws of perspective,' he said out of the corner of his mouth.

Biv cleared his throat. His Chief would give anything to meet *him*. He made a note.

'Then you'd know where the blessed cul-de-sac—'

'The locus in question is over yonder. I step down from here in a few minutes. I can take you.'

His place was taken by a gaunt figure wearing a yellow helmet who had perhaps the most arduous pose of all. The problem with the rest was to remain rigid. He, as an eminent seismologist, was expected to shake and vibrate for the full two hours. His name was Parkinson.

'He fell off not long ago,' said Biv's new friend. 'Broke an ankle.'

In keeping with the mysterious laws of perspective he and Biv were walking towards the horizon, gradually diminishing.

95

Find Biv before it is too late.

Stop him now.

If you can.

96

The slow movements of Grey's daughter. Hand moves in a series of pale arcs, performing tasks. To trace, (Biv, the draughtsman) would show interlocking trajectories expressed in volume, space, like a line drawing of overlapping motor tyres, pipes, parabola. The way, in a word, the mouth forms the slow crescent; cross-sections of her arms and thighs further circles; her breasts, floating oval circles; the navel, circular labyrinth; ohhs and ahhhhs; flexible, pulsating inner circle.

97

Biv asked, 'I've heard it said that God exists just below vanishing point. Have you come across that? Second, is the sky really a dome or sort of arched?'

'Ah, I don't know about your second question,' came the reply as they walked, 'and we're still working on the first.'

'I see. How far have you got? And, are we about near the cul-de-sac?'

'Ah, you've raised two separate questions there, but oddly enough they are related. We begin with a tree. Or take one of those telegraph poles. Now that one beside you is the same height as that one yonder. But it doesn't look it.'

98

His legs were tired. He wanted to rest.

Biv put up with a lot, but that is his way. It has its advantages. He was the one the Chief liked to confide in. Really, this Biv is quite a likeable character.

The Chief whacked him on the omoplates.

'There are many more enigmas in the shadow of a man who walks in the sun than all the religions of the past, present and future. Ah, straight from the great Giorgio de Chirico.' He was half drunk. Roy could see the man suffered from envy; had not got rid of it although he was now in his fifties. And he repeated himself. 'Before I forget, I have a tricky little job for you tomorrow. What a life. You and I are misunderstood.'

His beard was full of minestrone soup. He went outside and vomited. A minestrone mess with bitterness. He came back.

'You're all right, Roy. You'll do.'

To gauge temperature. In strategic locations volunteers in heavy fur coats stand barefoot in glass trays, the sides of the trays graduated like thermometers. By measuring the sweat level in the tray even someone ignorant of figures could tell at a glance if the climate was too hot or too cold. Without labouring the point, if it was freezing the tray of even the most heavily dressed volunteer would remain bone-dry. Students could do it for pocket money; ideal. Young pores are generally more mobile, extra sensitive! Yet the job would undoubtedly be dominated by large women or jockeys, quick to see they could be of some use to the community during their relentless efforts to reduce.

100

'There is no "country" as such,' the Chief liked to explain. ' "Country", or crust, is nothing more than an undulating base into which are screwed factories and other artificial protuber-ances, and'—the Chief waxing lyrical; no wonder he stood at the pinnacle of his profession—'laced over with bridges and wandering strips of cement we happen to call "highways", "country" is merely a bedrock, a base, which supports an econ-omy. We place and arrange things on the surface, including ourselves. Have you got that?

'These protuberances,' he said, tapping the table which was another protuberance, 'are the first to collect bullets, and are flattened during wars. The base, or the "country", remains more or less the same.'

101

A persistent, private vice which must now be obvious.

A tendency to wander. This is all right.

A conservative view of the opposite sex.

Add to that, deference to elders.

You have a good listener; by all appearances submissive, though not necessarily.

A cheery soul in the mornings.

Blue hands, orange hair. Watch strap held together by a rubber band.

Not a colourful character, but popular with the majority.

A casualness with socks, food stains and money; hypnotic to some.

He continues through force of habit.

102

Look at the scenery.

103

No wonder his legs, even his armpits, felt tired. He'd covered one and a half inches on the map. Still no sign of the ... Biv consulted the map. Was not exactly determined to get to the bottom of it but seemed to allow himself to be carried along by time and events, collective pressure from others, including the direction maps; and so forth. The optician followed at a discreet distance. 'Where are we? What about down there?' Biv shouted across. The optician blew his false nose and came over. He wore a pair of binoculars. 'See for yourself.'

The road was not twenty yards away yet it seemed to recede into the distance. Focusing, Biv saw a dusty path. Hardly a 'road' at all. It was dotted with limestone rocks. And skinny goats wandered between artificial thorn and olive trees.

'Down there,' said the optician, reading his mind, 'many a traveller is struck without warning by a bright light. It's a very odd thing. A person comes out a changed man. Certain scientists have had their Big Breakthroughs there. Inventors have been known to come running out shouting. The poet finds the right word. Sinners,' he added on a pious note, 'suddenly see the light.'

'No one's there now,' Biv remarked, scanning with the binoculars. 'And I don't see any bright light.'

'It's there, don't worry.' He added, 'And I'd get a move on.'

104

Biv wandering around. Another lost character. Fast losing perspective, among other things. The heel of the left shoe has worked loose and is flapping. From some angles Biv is pathetic.

105

There is a Library of Applied Noise: IF YOU WISH TO EMPHA-
SISE SOMETHING TAKE ONE NOW! A sneeze for sympathy, cries
of pain or alarm. Sighs of genuine misunderstanding, perhaps
a click of the tongue which in certain eastern countries means
'No'—borrow one of them. Heavy breathing. An adolescent's
belch. Angry hissing? Fright. Borrow some silence. Yes, a little
more silence from now on. First, help the young woman carry
out some laughter, it's spilling out onto the street, leaking,
both trying to hold it in, clutching and squashing.

106

On the left, a swamp. It lapped at his feet. Oh lord. Intricate
disorder ruffled the surface, inviting instant comparison. Statements floated. Some would remain unsinkable. Soggy words
kept sticking to the hands and face. He tried to keep balance.
It's always hard. In the mire, half hidden, stood a complex cat-
apulting machine, camouflaged, but obviously effective.

Behind was a sunset; a magnificent example by any standards. A corker of a sunset, a 'bobby dazzler'.

'One of the mysterious laws of perspective,' said his friend
with a nod of the head, but keeping his eyes firmly ahead, 'is
that *left* indicates the past and individual characteristics, and
right indicates the future. A recent discovery, though it's more
in the realm of Psychology. There is also the interesting fact
that pedestrians in the Southern Hemisphere veer towards the
left, while in the Northern they stick to the right. This, of

course, is the effect of Coriolis forces. We also know'—continuing for Biv's edification—'that the left and right legs of a horse consist of twenty-four consecutive triangles when the animal gallops. Therefore a leg is not always a leg, though that is more in the realm of Optical Physiology.'

Biv frowned. They seemed to be walking in the one spot.

'I'd like to know,' he said, 'why we close our eyes during pain, pleasure or physical effort? It often enters my head.'

'That's one for the optician,' his friend countered. 'Better ask him.'

Biv turned. He saw a crowd following. One of the rat traps in his pocket went off. He began running.

'In short, the cul-de-sac is determined by its entry point which is short. In short—'

107

She was allowing it then, she was going ahead with it. The window was wide open. Hoisting himself up and balancing he could see her dressing-table, her combs and brushes. From the next room came the click-clicking of Grey's trains. This fence was rotten. It was covered in moss. He began vibrating to keep balance; he felt himself reddening.

108

Slid the set square along to the width (proportional) of the street. Sharpened the pencil. Resumed. Repeated parallel towards the blank area of the cul-de-sac...Blue Staedtler (the most beautiful pencil; ask any—) firm against the bevelled perspex. The Staedtler blue. Is it hexagonal? Five, six. Hexagonal, it is. His purple fingers on the flat, white paper. The drawing board sloped down, and there, touched his knee.

Up front the Chief gesticulating to someone in his glass office.

A, B, C, D, E, F, G, H, I, J, K, L, M, N, O, P, Q, R, S, T, U, V, W, X, Y, Z

I select from these letters, pressing my fingers down. The letter (or an image of it) appears on the sheet of paper. It signifies little or nothing, I have to add more. Other letters are placed alongside until a 'word' is formed. And it is not always the word WORD.

The word matches either my memory of its appearance, or a picture of the object the word denotes. TREE: I see the shape of a tree at mid-distance, and green.

I am writing a story.

Here, the trouble begins.

The word 'dog', as William James pointed out, does not bite; and my story begins with a weeping woman. She sat at my kitchen table one afternoon and wept uncontrollably. How can words, particularly 'wept uncontrollably', convey her sadness (her self-pity)? Philosophers other than myself have discussed the inadequacy of words. 'Woman' covers women of every shape and size, whereas the one I have in mind is red-haired, has soft arms, plain face, high-heeled shoes with shining straps.

And she was weeping.

Her name, let us say, is Kathy Pridham.

For the past two years she has worked as a librarian for the British Council in Karachi. She, of all the British community there, was one of the few who took the trouble to learn Urdu, the local language. She could speak it, not read it: those calligraphic loops and dots meant nothing to her, except that 'it was a language'. Speaking it was enough. The local staff at the Council, shopkeepers, and even the cream of Karachi society (who cultivated European manners), felt that she knew them as they themselves did.

At this point, consider the word 'Karachi'. Not having been there myself I see clusters of white-cube buildings with the edge of a port to the left, a general slowness, a shaded verandah-ed suburb for the Burra sahibs. Perhaps, eventually, boredom—or disgust with noises and smells not understood. Kathy, who was at firstly lonely and disturbed, quickly settled in. She became fully occupied and happy; insofar as that word has any meaning. There was a surplus of men in Karachi: young English bachelors sent out from head office, and pale appraising types who worked at the embassies; but the ones who fell over themselves to be near her were Pakistanis. They were young and lazy. With her they were ardent and gay.

Already the words Kathy and Karachi are becoming inextricably linked.

It was not long before she too was rolling her head in slow

motion during conversations, and clicking her tongue, as they did, to signify 'no'. Her bungalow in the European quarter with its lawn, verandah, two archaic servants, became a sort of *salon*, especially at the Sunday lunches where Kathy reigned, supervising, flitting from one group to the next. Those afternoons never seemed to end. No one wanted to leave. Sometimes she had musicians perform. And there was always plenty of liquor (imported), with wide dishes of hot food. Kathy spoke instantly and volubly on the country's problems, its complicated politics, yet in London if she had an opinion she had rarely expressed it.

When Kathy thought of London she often saw 'London'— the six letters arranged in recognisable order. Then parts of an endless construction appeared, much of it badly blurred. There was the thick stone. Concentrating, she could recall a familiar bus stop, the interior of a building where she had last worked. Her street invariably appeared, strangely dead. Some men in overcoats. It was all so far away she sometimes thought it existed only when she was there. Her best friends had been two women; one a schoolteacher; the other married to a taciturn engineer. With them she went to Scotland for holidays, to the concerts at Albert Hall. Karachi was different. The word stands for something else.

The woman weeping at the kitchen table is Kathy Pridham. It is somewhere in London (there are virtually no kitchen tables in Karachi).

After a year or so Kathy noticed at a party a man standing apart from the others, watching her. His face was bony and fierce, and he had a thin moustache. Kathy, of course, turned away, yet at the same time tilted her chin and began acting over-earnest in conversation. For she pictured her appearance: seeing it (she thought) from his eyes.

She noticed him at other parties, and at one where she knew the host well enough casually asked, 'Tell me. Who is that over there?'

They both looked at the man watching her.

'If you mean him, that's Syed Masood. Not your cup of tea, Kathy. What you would call a wild man.' The host was a successful journalist and drew in on his cigarette. 'Perhaps he is our best painter. I don't know; I have my doubts.'

Kathy lowered her eyes, confused.

When she looked up, the man called Syed Masood had gone.

Over the next few days, she went to the galleries around town and asked to see the paintings of Syed Masood. She was interested in local arts and crafts, and had decided that if she saw something of his she liked she would buy it. These gallery owners threw up their hands. 'He has released nothing for two years now. What has got into him I don't know.'

Somehow this made Kathy smile.

Ten or eleven days pass—in words that take only seconds to put down, even less to absorb (the discrepancy between time and language). It is one of her Sunday lunches. Kathy is only half-listening to conversations and when she breaks into laughter it is a fraction too loud. She has invited this man Masood and has one eye on the door. He arrives late. Perhaps he too is nervous.

Their opening conversation (aural) went something like this (visual).

'Do come in. I don't think we've met. My name is Kathy Pridham.'

'Why do you mix with all these shits?' he replied looking around the room.

Just then an alarm wristlet watch on one of the young men began ringing. Everyone laughed, slapping each other, except Masood.

'I'll get you something,' said Kathy quietly. 'You're probably hungry.'

She felt hot and awkward, although now that they were together he seemed to take no notice of her. Several of the European men came over, but Masood didn't say much and they drifted back. She watched him eat and drink: the bones of his face working.

He finally turned to her. 'You come from—where?'

'London.'

'Then why have you come here?'

She told him.

'And these?' he asked, meaning the crowd reclining on cushions.

'My friends. They're people I've met here.'

Suddenly she felt like crying. But he took her by the shoulders. 'What is this? You speak Urdu? And not at all bad? Say something more, please.'

Before she could think of anything he said in a voice that disturbed her, 'You are something extraordinary.' He was so close she could feel his breath. 'Do you know that? Of course. But do you know how extraordinary? Let me tell you something, although another man might put it differently. It begins here'—for a second one of his many hands touched her breasts; Kathy jumped—'and it emanates. Your volume fills the room. Certainly! So you are quite vast, but beautiful.'

Then he added, watching her, 'If you see what I mean.'

He was standing close to her, but when he spoke again she saw him grinning. 'Now repeat what I have just said in Urdu.'

He made her laugh.

Here—now—an interruption. While considering the change in Kathy's personality I remember an incident from last Thursday, the 12th. This is an intrusion but from 'real life'. The words in the following paragraph reconstruct the event as remembered. As accurately as possible, of course.

A beggar came up to me in a Soho bar and asked (a hoarse whisper) if I wished to see photographs of funerals. I immediately pictured a rectangular hole, sky, men and women in coats. Without waiting for my reply he fished out from an inside pocket the wad of photographs, postcard size, each one of a burial. They were dog-eared and he had dirty fingernails. 'Did you know these dead people?' He shook his head. 'Not even their names?' He shook his head. 'That one,' he said, not taking his eyes off the photographs, 'was dug yesterday. That one, in 1969.' There was little difference. Both showed men and women standing around a dark rectangle, perplexed. I felt a sharp tap on my wrist. The beggar had his hand out. Yes, I gave him a shilling. The barman spoke: 'Odd way to earn a living. He's been doing that for—'

Kathy soon saw Masood again. He arrived one night with his shirt hanging out while she was entertaining the senior British Council representative, Mr L and his wife. They were a cautious experienced pair, years in the service, yet Mrs L began talking loudly and hastily, a sign of indignation, when Masood sat away from the table, silently watching them. Mr L cleared his throat several times—another sign. It was a hot night with both ceiling fans hardly altering the sedentary air. Masood suddenly spoke to Kathy in his own language. She nodded and poured him another coffee. Mrs L caught her husband's eye, and when they left shortly afterwards Kathy and Masood leaned forward and leaned back and laughed.

'You can spell my name four different ways,' Masood declared in the morning, 'but I am still the one person! Ah,' he said laughing. 'I am in a good mood. This is an auspicious day.'

'I have to go to work,' said Kathy.

'Look up "auspicious" when you get to the library. See what it says in one of your English dictionaries.'

She bent over to fit her brassière. Her body was marmoreal, the opposite to his: bony and nervy.

'Instead of thinking of me during the day,' he went on, 'think of an exclamation mark! It amounts to the same thing. I would see you, I think, as a colour. Yes, I think more than likely pink, or something soft like yellow.'

'You can talk,' said Kathy laughing.

But she liked hearing him talk. Perhaps there'll be further examples of why she enjoyed hearing him talk.

That night Masood took her into his studio. It was in the inner part of the city where Europeans rarely ventured, and as Masood strode ahead Kathy avoided, but not always successfully, the stares of women in doorways, the fingers of beggars, and rows of sleeping bodies. She noticed how some men deliberately dawdled or bumped into her; striding ahead, Masood seemed to enjoy having her there. In an alleyway he unbolted a powder-blue door as a curious crowd gathered. He suddenly clapped his hands to move them. Then Kathy was inside: a fluorescent room, dirty whitewashed walls. In the corner was a wooden bed called a 'charpoy', some clothes over a chair. There were brushes in jars, and tins of paint.

'Syed, are these your pictures?'

'Leave them,' he said sharply. 'Come here. I would like to see you.'

Through the door she could feel the crowd in the alleyway. She was perspiring still and now he was undoing her blouse.

'Syed, let's go?'

He stepped back.

'What is the matter? The natives are too dirty tonight. Is that it? Yes, the walls; the disgusting size of the place. All this stench. It must be affecting your nostrils? Rub your nose in it. Lie in my shit and muck. If you wait around you might see a rat. You could dirty your memsahib's hands for a change.' Then he kicked his foot through one of the canvases by the door. 'The pretty paintings you came to see.'

As she began crying she wondered why. (He was only a person who used certain words.)

I will continue with further words.

Kathy made room for Masood in her house, in her bed as well as the spare room which she made his studio. Her friends noticed a change. At work, they heard the pronoun 'we' constantly. She told them of parties they went to, the trips they planned to take, how she supervised his meals; she even confessed (laughing) he snored and possessed a violent temper. At parties, she took to sitting on the floor. She began wearing 'kurtas' instead of 'blouses', 'lungis' rather than 'dresses', even though with her large body she looked clumsy. To the Europeans she somehow became, or seemed, untidy. They no longer understood her, and so they felt sorry for her. It was about then that Kathy's luncheon parties stopped, and she and Masood, who were always together, went out less frequently. Most people saw Masood behind this—he had never disguised his contempt for her friends—but others connected it with an incident at the office. Kathy arrived one morning wearing a sari and was told by the chief librarian it was inappropriate; she couldn't serve at the counter wearing that. Then Mr L himself, rapidly consulting his wife, spoke to her. He spelt out the *British* Council's function in Karachi, underlining the word British. 'Kathy, are you happy?' he suddenly asked. Like others, he was concerned. He wanted to say, 'Do you know what you are doing?' 'Oh, yes,' Kathy replied. 'With this chap, I mean,' he said, waving his hand. And Kathy left the room.

People's distrust of Masood seemed to centre around his unconventional appearance and (perhaps more than anything) his rude silences. Nobody could say they knew him, although just about everybody said he drank too much. Stories began circulating. 'A surly bugger,' he was called behind his back. That was common now. There were times when he cursed Kathy in public. Strange, though, the wives and other women were more ready to accept the affair. There was something about Masood, his face and manner. And they recognised the tenacity with which Kathy kept living with him. They understood her quick defence of him, often silent but always there, even when she came late to work, puff-eyed from crying and once, her cheek bruised.

Here, the life of Kathy draws rapidly to a close.

It was now obvious to everyone that Masood was drinking too much. At the few parties they attended he usually made a scene of some sort; and Kathy would take him home. Think of swear words. She was arriving late for work and missed whole days. Then she disappeared for a week. They had argued one night and Kathy screamed at him to leave. He replied by hitting her across the mouth. She moved into a cheap hotel, but within the week he found her. 'Syed spent all day, every day, looking for me,' was how she later put it. 'He needs someone.' When she was reprimanded for her disappearance and general conduct, she burst into tears.

In London, the woman with elbows on the table is Kathy Pridham. She has unwrapped a parcel from Karachi. Imagine: coarse screwed-up paper and string lie on the table. Masood has sent a self-portrait, oil on canvas, quite a striking resemblance. His vanity, pride and troubles are enormous. His face, leaning against the teapot, stares across at Kathy weeping.

She cannot help thinking of him; of his appearance.

Words. These marks on paper, and so on.

The Partitions

Ross is good, there is no doubt about that. Channon is better
though. Strong calves and confidence. To see them soaring
over the first. They set a tremendous example. The others follow clattering and adjusting like pigeons, eyes ahead, two
bright patches among the dark-suits women, elbowing like
Currumbin parrots, their wings clipped. These positions will
not, cannot, last. The world consists of inter-reacting particles,
the ever-changing pattern a cause of much bafflement. Occasionally concern.

At the usual height of five foot five the partitions follow
the perimeter of the building forming cubicles. Some cream-
coloured, others green.

Most of plywood, sanded glass, though every now and
then one in imitation teak or such. Parts were rickety. On top
of the partitions, dust. Dead flies there and further along

someone had left drawing pins (almost calculated to puncture hands).

It was a cracking pace.

Channon, Ross.

Then Purley. He was thirty-three, a three-piece suit, so he looked nothing like Christ. Besides, he wore a yellow wedding ring and two others (making three). A shade too eager. Purley wore flash shoes. The others could see the tan soles flicking back slippery.

Beginning on the left a 'typists' pool', though scarcely a glance was possible. The thing was to keep moving, the chief difficulty being simple balance. Slip, a pause, meant permanent loss of position. Girls in uniform sat rubbing and blowing their typewriters, and one who didn't was filing and blowing her fingernails. A man slipped (noticing this). Purley, Miles, Bess who was Channon's devoted wife, then Stubbs, Jeanette McColl, young Wozley, P. S. Spickett holding his tennis racquet, Kondratieff, a few others, and Kemp passed the first partitions OK.

Barely settled down when this.

Ross wore a red carnation in an attempt to associate him with, yet distinguish him from, the powerful leader Channon, who wore red elastic braces. Young Wozley pointed ahead, 'Look, Mr Ross is losing his petals!' They were coming back, yes, into people's eyes, were found squashed along the tops of the partitions. Already then. Some sort of struggle up ahead. Enough to spur them on as if the petals were the first signs of blood, Purley especially, third, whose action in the new shoes became a scramble. Miles went up alongside. Easy. Passing a cubicle which had an ordinary filing cabinet and venetian blinds. Balancing on a chair, his back to them, stood a man adjusting the hands of a clock large enough to serve a railway station (the clock).

On all fours passing, tintinnabulation.

At this stage already some were looking good. That is to say, holding something in reserve. People like Miles have the momentum of freight trains, watch, crashing through the gates, following the route laid down. Stubbs behind him, *subtle*. Therefore ambitious. Generally considered to be, yes. Apparent casualness a trademark. Unlike Miles he wore a coat, and no ballpoints protruding from his shirt. Stubbs however was glancing at Jeanette McColl. Her mannequin's throat! Model teeth! P. S. Spickett in the middle watched them draw ahead. Little is ever known about Spickett, watch.

Imagination is costly on the partitions. To keep moving meant a reduction in politeness, even kindness. Naturally to advance requires a number of victims.

From Channon in front expressions of alarm suddenly appeared, face by face. The partitions here loose. To a crawl, single file, the wood creaking under the hands. To make matters worse some of the fluorescent tubes missing. Apparently a storage area hardly ever used. Cubicles there stacked with wrong plans and forecasts, discarded arrows, rulers a shade too short, at least a dozen useless chairs.

Broken chairs. And the man adjusting the clock, back there, suddenly fell from his. A leg had snapped. His head struck the corner of the desk.

Kemp lying last, now he must have seen this but kept quiet. He shouldn't have been there anyway (Kemp). A good two feet shorter than Spickett, he wore a straw hat, an old bow tie. He was on tablets (man prodded along by an invisible hand), Kemp.

The line lengthened by the half dark squashed and bulged again. The partitions improved, perhaps recently repaired. Channon chose that moment to relax, unusual for him, to glance back at his wife. Showing off? She tried to shout with her eyes. The rest gasped. Ross slipped past on the inside.

It threw Channon. And Purley moved up almost alongside. Channon's flabbergasted face sent murmurs down the line. The archetype now merely bad tempered, flustered. The ease!

Swarmed past an office almost without it registering. A man there looking out a window. Wozley twisted around, he must have been imagining things. 'Isn't that my old man? He's bald. Yes, it's Dad!' Miss McColl gave him a smile. Little he could do. Once on the partitions difficult to get off. Wozley was pushed on by the others. They were above the next cubicle, a small one spotted with postcards. The paraphernalia stuffed in the cubicles, or the way it's arranged, shows the personality of the occupant in effect. Clicketty-clack. There a solitary typist on a swivel chair examined her breast. Oh Jesus. Her blouse unbuttoned, the soft thing spilling out of her hand, and the one who'd slipped earlier crashed right off the partitions, shaking the line. Stubbs almost lost that fine balance too. Miss McColl turned sharply away from the girl. Old Kondratieff held his tremulous half smile through this and everything. Kondratieff, who allowed himself to be carried along like a leaf on a wave.

Clacketty-clack.

'Are you all right? Are you telling me the truth?' Mrs

Channon wanted to ask her husband, eyes on him. Puffing and anxious to pass Miles and Purley she showed a profile the epitome of elegance, dust on her neck like some new cosmetic applied to emphasise loyalty, concern for the future. Worried for Channon. His head grew tomato red. They passed a cubicle filled with windows which were actually mirrors. Something wrong along here. Perhaps someone had turned the air-conditioning off? Miss McColl dropped her stilettos, all wet, while others loosened their ties. A queer invisible slope here measured by the paraplegic action of Purley, his slipping and clawing transmitted back, each one catching the disease, to Kemp, who would find this 'slope' difficult indeed. A drawer glided out from the filing cabinet. Trays, papers began to slide. Not long before Purley slipped like the pencil on one of the desks (due to his shoes?), tearing his suit, and this is a problem with the partitions, fell into Miles and Mrs Channon, sending them against Stubbs, McColl, young muttering Wozley, into Spickett, each depending on the other, shouting, for to fall was the end, those who had managed to return were never the same.

Relative silence as they fought to extricate.

Stubbs set out after the leaders, soon followed by McColl, not bothering to dust herself, then the rest. Rapid recovery, re-silience, rank among the prerequisites, though with her she wanted to be near Stubbs, he wore spotless underwear, was the type, no pee drops. She found this attractive in a man. The leaders fifteen, twenty yards ahead.

Back in sixth Mrs Channon had P. S. Spickett and his tennis racquet at her elbow. 'P. S.' could have been his nickname. The hissing came from asthma or breathing through his teeth.

Her determined face suddenly cried out. Spickett trod on her hand without a word, magnifying his silence (which worried everybody), illustrating the situation more or less on the partitions.

The first corner up ahead.

Ross, Channon and Miles turned right, large and close for a second, before the hypotenuse formed by Mrs Channon's gaze rapidly lengthened. 'Charles?' she whispered across. 'Be careful. And I was going to tell you.'

She stopped. A kind of helplessness had entered his movements, and on all fours, stubbornly ignoring the crowd, somehow made it worse.

'Poor thing,' Miss McColl ventured to Stubbs.

Stubbs put his hand inside her blouse. 'Yes,' he said. 'I feel sorry for her too.'

They turned the corner.

'For goodness sake,' Stubbs shouted. 'The dirty bastard.'

Channon banging—four blurry emissions—blowing back the skirts of his jacket. Yet all along self-control was supposed to be his specialty. The disgust! Miles directly behind shoved past, holding his nose, and surprised at how easy, or out of contempt, gave Channon a push with one foot. Flurry of limbs as he fought to stay on, while they watched (he was holding them up).

Yet on Mrs Channon the effect was one of softening, now why is that? A matter of release. Simply the skin below her mouth sagged, she seemed to lose interest and weight at once.

Lavatories below, one by one, and one occupied by a man, trousers down, reading the paper and sipping coffee from a Wedgwood cup. To look down certainly a temptation on the partitions. Their shadows too performed eye-catching patterns along the wall reminiscent of Japanese wrestling, contemporary dancing, perhaps even copulation. Mrs Channon tried smiling at this. Someone should have warned her, Kondratieff being the closest. The rest were watching her husband clambering, or trying to, ahead.

Now, look, one front foot missed the wooden strip. Mrs Channon fell. She grabbed to hold and both elbows went through the glass. Sssshib, bang and crack. Her face hovered there like a child's. With her weight pulling down, her mouth and eyes slowly opened wide. The points had converged, not a word.

Those following stopped. Stubbs and McColl came back. Kemp took off his hat. The clatter of the three ahead seemed distant, unrelated. Obviously Channon went on not knowing who it was. Yes, some raised their hands to call out. Then Spickett was seen trying to edge past McColl, to gain a place and it triggered them off, tintinnabulation, to clatter of hail on a roof, steadying.

Ross and Miles drew well ahead.

Looking good, etc., as might be expected.

These two were the first to reach the large seemingly endless cubicle.

Cubicles within cubicles, partitions interlocking forming additional cubicles, dead ends, apparently endless patterns of partitions. Ross disappeared. Rather, kept 'reappearing' in it.

In five or six seconds, if that, Miles turned to find his way back. He took a pair of pliers from his back pocket as if that'd help.

Old Channon there came out ahead of both, Channon's illogical state of mind suited to this. Fixing that point, avoiding Miles towards the centre, the rest found a path in effect, tail-enders swallowing up Miles (scratching his head). Now from Ross to the rest an arm's length if that. Apparent superiority is modified by time, 'external factors'. See that.

Ross got past Channon again.

This revealed to the rest the protuberant state of Channon's head, his swelling legs. How even his fingers were incredibly red.

'Where are we going? What is our position? I would like to answer that by quoting, if I may, last year's figures. Under the most difficult conditions we managed—'

In a carpeted cubicle a man before a mirror pulled a variety of faces. He looked like Channon before, or Ross. (He wore a red carnation.) He suddenly beamed.

'Due to your continuous efforts we managed a gross IN-CREASE of approximately .6 per cent. A very fine effort indeed, believe me.'

After testing a number of different smiles he went close to the mirror to examine his chin. He stood back, raising his voice.

'With such application shown in the past you may well ask, where will our position lie in the future? And you have every right to ask. Which reminds me. Did you hear the one about? . . .'

A cry from Ross in front. His hands had met the drawing pins. Both hands, look, studded with gold. By quickly stopping he imagined he could remove the pins, but Channon was banged into him, sending him on, waving violently for balance. Under no illusions then. The same force carried McColl over, her bare feet luckily only caressing the partitions, and was fondled airborne by Stubbs. His hand moved up her skirt.

All eyes on Ross however.

Some empty cubicles, and one filled with stuff like dandruff, skin from worn elbows.

A right angle ahead, these partitions follow the walls, remember. Its significance apparently lost on Ross, he slowed to turn. The rest accelerated, propelling him straight on, protesting, down a 'siding'. Simultaneously Channon muddled through, a dead horse or inflatable beach toy in heavy surf.

Channon again leader.

So now P. S. Spickett saw his chance. Jumping the corner, normally not advisable on the partitions, he took second. Just then Stubbs and McColl were too entangled to resist. Each change in positions watched by the majority, sometimes with bitterness.

Kemp said something.

'Don't waste your breath,' said Kondratieff.

The line slowed considerably, clattering merely a drumming, part shuffle, with it the difficulty of keeping balance. Not all the fault of Channon, however. Most were glancing below, each bumping into the other. On the desk a woman lay back, legs apart, receiving a man. His trousers over a chair. Her teeth and hands opening and closing in time. Why at that point did Miss McColl begin the steady weeping? Others, the laughing? The man on the desk was too hairy, the woman skinny. And in a small antechamber a crowd watched through a hole, tiptoe, hands on each other's shoulders.

Three, four tastefully furnished cubicles.

Breathing spaces.

In five a store of proven to be successful words, labelled, ready to use (ALRIGHTY, WITH KINDEST REGARDS, FUCKWIT, JESUS CHRIST, ETC., PARTITIONS).

Some weaknesses in the legs by then. Each one still eyeing the other however.

Channon! Spickett now shoving and poking with his tennis racquet. That Spickett all ready and grinning. The flaccid prisoner in front almost bursting asunder from the suit buttoned up at all costs.

Scarcely noticing the long room passing. Wiry priests and lay preachers exercised over padded boxes, jumping up and down, performing superb perpendicular somersaults, some balancing on their heads. Their gymnasium by the look. The noise doubling the din in effect. Producing tinnitus in Kemp. Bang, bang, cracking jokes in the midst of spinning somersaults (repeated). Their black shapes spin interestingly against the stationary white background.

Channon began flailing the light bulbs hanging down, blaming them, but there was something more fundamentally wrong. Either his body was at the end of its tether, or the distortions were due to frustration or rage. He should have stopped, look.

Spickett moved to pass, everyone watching.

Channon now fumbled oddly, however, some buttons fell off, and like the toadfish found in St Vincent Gulf gasped and exploded. Blood, intestines and cloth flew over them, liver and bits of red nose hit the ceiling. Spickett caught the full force. His empty spot on the partitions drenched, his voice somewhere in the corridor below right. The line momentarily off balance recovered and went on, sometimes slipping, whenever possible wiping themselves with handkerchiefs.

'For the phenomenon to continue a certain amount of symmetry should be absent.' Yes, at least keep going. Understand.

Passing a crowd in numbered chairs, backs to the partitions, who suddenly applauded. A few laughed, confused. Miss McColl touched up her hair.

Enough to smarten them up, just like that, for the rhythm to pick up. Clacketty-clack! Each one noticing the years, but continuing. These partitions cannot go on forever. That was understood. Stubbs, look, drawing ahead. He set a tremendous example.

Ahead all dark bar the bright patch shining, it made them blink. Chrome, stainless steel and linoleum appeared below. The table apparently set for a family. Lids happened to vibrate on a stove, the lids connected to underground pipes in effect. Hence to various saliva ducts, swichh, snap, snkk. On the wall an old calendar for Heidelberg Printing Machinery. The refrigerator electric, of 21 cu. ft. capacity (Miles noticed, he knew).

Old Kemp began coughing.

'Come on,' said Kondratieff.

No one could see Stubbs ahead. Night personified up ahead. Jeanette McColl called out, and all they heard was the faint applause behind like a rattle. The emptiness in effect. Each and everyone shouting. To her to pipe down, shut up. Just hurry on.

Approaching the last.

A faint glow to show the way, if that, this cubicle like a

bedroom, almost exactly, crepuscular shafts leaking from a tin lamp above the bed. A pair were about to retire, to rejuvenate. He, facing the vast wardrobe, stroking his chin with his fingertips, fat stomach and cock hanging down. A slow body by the look but with the usual momentum. Standing on a carpet of dead (trodden on) roses. She handed him an alarm clock to wind.

Probably most then wanted to hurry past but this was not possible in the dark.

The woman sat up and began pulling hairs out from her nose with tweezers.

The partitions at intervals creaking. Their own breathing another powerful sound. They wanted to find the end before she switched off the lamp. The man climbed into bed. A scene which seemed to recede an inch at a time.

He sat up remembering something. Slippers. He took them out of the bed and placed them on the floor.

The horizontal movement altered to that of dropping, one by one, to the floor. A pause to dust themselves, adjust a tie. The odd remark or two seemed appropriate here and there. Some had coats of special waterproof material. Each and every one stepping out closing the door.

Home Ownership

The insidious Habit of Thrift was proclaimed by the churches and the home-purchase pamphlets: '13,690 homes have been provided, another 605 are under construction.' That was the year ending 30 June 1934. All you needed was a deposit of £35. The houses were built on ironbark stilts, Brisbane being such a humid city. It's the stilts and the galvanised iron which give Brisbane its temporary air as if the whole lot could be quickly dismantled or swept away.

The street began like all the rest littered with sharp-smelling sawdust and bent nails not yet rusty or trodden into the ground. The sewerage came later. All white, the row of wooden houses exuded a kind of transparent hope, definitely, like new glass. The ground all around was bare.

That was—what? Goodness, forty years back.

Like everything else, the street has changed.

Number 17 has the front porch converted into a sleep-out with louvred windows. Next door there, 'EMOH RUO', has the yellow carport leaning against the side.

Plenty of others have tacked on, if not another bedroom, something. There are metal blinds galore, house names in inlaid mulga, portholes, lantern-lights near the doorbell, various weathervanes and ornamental flyscreens.

After the war the street went through a slack phase; nothing much moved (changed). A nomadic period followed, rented accommodation, the appearance of solitary strangers.

And now—must be due to the exorbitant cost of new housing—young couples have returned, and there's been a spate of further extensions, 'improvements', shouting children at dusk, powersaws biting into the night. Only one house, Parker's there over the road, has remained as it was, motionless on its stilts, while the street and time passed it by. Parker couldn't be better named! Since he moved in the week after he married he hasn't budged.

As a young man he rode a bike to work, the future before him. In those days he had yellow hair and an open blank expression. With their new house in the background Joyce would run out and wave, after first wiping her hands on her thighs: funny characteristic habit of hers. Then she'd remain for several minutes leaning over the gate, looking up and down. Other times, early in their marriage, she could be seen digging in the garden with a heart-shaped trowel.

Joyce cut back the wild grass and muck; carted away the builder's rubbish; and one weekend had Parker out there pouring concrete borders. Here she planted several cactus plants which threw geometric shadows at dusk. It was an attempt to impose order on the harsh elements, as if their lives would become ordered accordingly. This is common in Queensland. People dress very neatly.

Yet Joyce certainly wasn't the person one normally associates with cactus. The house wore brightly coloured curtains. On certain afternoons the windows reflected the trees and passing clouds just like her sunglasses, while the door in between kept opening and closing. With the step painted verandah-red, the house had a look... very conscious of itself. Joyce had this other funny habit, noticeable even from a distance. After saying something, usually to a man, she'd roll her lips back as if she'd committed an error or was applying lipstick. A nervous habit. She was short, firm-breasted. She had large eyes. Oh, she was something! Joyce always liked to laugh. At the same time she was serious she could be hard on Parker some days—waiting for him the minute he stepped in. He, the pedalling Methodist, without a tie but with the top button done up. He had a simple wooden expression. It implied stubbornness. Where did they meet? A ludicrous doomed pair. Couldn't everyone see that?

Brisbane hummed with a kind of humid emptiness. It drove people with a perfectly sound mind to drink. The slow-moving days were punctuated at metronomic intervals by door-to-door salesmen. The ring on Parker's bell was the signal, though often as not the house would be wide open.

The house breathed through the door.

'I say, anybody home? You-who!'

And then came the murmur of Joyce's time-consuming idle questions; at intervals her sudden high laugh.

There was nothing else to do in Brisbane.

Raising one trousered leg on the stop, arms and jaws all working in unison, the reps altered the geometry of the foreground. Most of them were hardworking with mortgages of their own, and it was noticeable how after a while most of them took to avoiding Joyce's door. She never bought a thing.

There was one particular regular who peddled American pens and propelling pencils, all colours, in rows like picket fences. His narrow sample-case was lined with them.

This man had a hungry tanned neck, wiry wrists—loose gold watch—and wore brown suit-trousers. He had lizard eyes. The eyes of a lizard: sliding off while selling halfheartedly, more interested in her over the road bending in the garden. He let out a loud conspiratorial laugh without foundation, and Joyce glanced up. You could see what he was up to. Few weeks later, sure enough, he was in there, leg up on the step, his suitcase of pens not even opened. Shielding her eyes, Joyce had a way of squinting: her hand apexed over eyes duplicated the shape of the peaked roof sheltering the windows.

Every second Thursday he called. Regular as clockwork.

He liked to say, 'I'll toddle off now to Mrs Cactus,' and wink. He called her Mrs Cactus.

A familiarity did grow between them. He was a traveller of sorts. He had endless stories. She took to sitting casually, ostentatiously, on his suitcase, exposing the red step of the open door. Clasping one knee as they did in those days, she leaned back and laughed. Some afternoons she wore pale-blue shorts.

He told lies about himself, lies a woman recognises and yet laughs. They were for her.

She liked to laugh.

With Parker she didn't have much of a chance.

Some Friday afternoons he began appearing without calling on other houses; and every other Thursday Joyce would be there wandering casually around near the gate, expectant. Coatless in summer, leaning against the house, that shirt of his merged with the white weatherboard. All that was visible then was his tanned head. She'd come out with what looked like lime cordial or tea. For several hours he'd stay. Parker usually worked overtime on Fridays. And the house with its picket fence maintained a dental smile, no sign of decay. There was nothing much wrong with what they were doing—sitting on the steps—yet the women who'd liked Joyce before seemed to think so. They shied away and pulled faces at the slightest pretext. Perhaps they were right; because Joyce took no notice. And no longer did he bother even bringing his sample-case. It turned out later he had lost his job.

Strange how 1939, fateful year for the world, was on a smaller scale a fateful year for the Parkers.

Underneath these Brisbane houses people store their tools and ladders, fruit for preserves, bits of timber and junk in shadows bordered by the stilts. To camouflage the mess, white lattice covers the front and sides, perforating the shadows. It's dark and cool underneath.

At about four one afternoon he emerged from there, and

returned casually to his place on the steps. A little later Joyce followed and went inside. He turned to say something, but she had shut the door. The exact day is easily remembered. Hitler's armies had poured into Poland, a Friday.

Emptied, made plain, devastated by the war, the street like many others in Brisbane took an age to recover. The street seemed wider, but of course it wasn't.

Parker's house was still there; it seemed to have tilted slightly. This was another optical illusion. The undergrowth and the turbulent dead sticks which had been allowed to go wild after Joyce's death formed shoulders across the foreground, obliterating the stilts and lattice, one shoulder higher than the other. It came as a shock: it had overwhelmed Joyce's cactus, darkened the face of the house. Nothing had been done to lift the fallen front gutter, and the first time it rained, in 1945, it shed three separate streams of water.

Joyce had been pregnant, as everybody knew. Poor girl. She was found in the bathroom, sometime early 1940. Circumstances remain vague. But complications occurred more in those days. Parker, of course, had always wanted children, actually talking about five. He was a fool.

Joyce was twenty-eight.

The front door had opened and closed a few times, then it remained shut. There was no light. Parker preferred the back, the kitchen, at night.

His punctuality became a joke. He hardly spoke. With its hooded eyes, jowls, resting on its dry shoulders, the house stubbornly gazed. It was always there. Lily-white in Joyce's day, its complexion beginning to deteriorate, the former pink-ish glow at the end of the day assuming a kind of ashen grey. Unattended, the paint-skin began falling away, in Parker's case revealing raw patches; it can be the problem with weather-boards. The red step, that characteristic spot alive in the centre, chafed and faded. No longer was it the focal point. Nothing was. At five o'clock a slate-coloured shadow grew below the windows and spread, and over the years darkened consider-ably.

Parker stopped going to church. He over-reacted, it was said.

Dandruff spotted his shoulders. He had filled out consid-erably: wide dark shoulders. His hair thinned and turned a kind of rust-brown. Short, back and sides. When he came out and stumbled along unshaven, unkempt, it was with his kitbag to buy groceries. Some of his front teeth had gone.

It was said he had gone soft in the head.

The eyebrows darkened as weeds grew and withered in the gutter, drooping over the twin miniature roofs shading the front windows. These jutted either with stubbornness or a kind of blindness. The windows beneath retreated into the shadows, never cleaned. The frown which developed was caused there by the line of wooden slats above the windows, and the angle of the fallen main gutter. Slowly the picket fence lost its smile. It had always been inane, irritating, anyway. Pal-ings turned grey and here and there loosened by humidity and time angled and fell away: dark spaces, gaping holes, were dis-played. Sometime in the fifties Parker had to wear glasses. Parker had an unusually lined and weathered face for his age. As time passes, it takes an effort to maintain appearances.

Grey weeds appeared, most noticeably out of the chimney.

The nose seemed to lengthen. They do with age. It grew dark, a blue-grey, and in the morning dripped for several hours.

Parker didn't seem to care.

Parker seemed merely to continue, passing through the house and time. It was a life.

Perhaps inevitably, the plumbing gave trouble. Quite an operation digging around the foundations; quite a stench, too, of soaked earth and ruptured pipes. It had to be done.

Parker had hardly missed a day's work in his life.

There was the Vietnam war in the late sixties.

Certainly, the roof showed signs of age. Apart from the gutters which suddenly overflowed without control or warning, a few of the corrugated sheets and the ridge-cap lifted in the slightest breeze, and rust, first freckles, then beer-coloured streaks became dark scabs: another darkening process. The roof was eggshell thin. And of course early on parts of the lattice had gaping holes, evidently rotten below the shoulders, like one of Parker's Swedish singlets.

He withdrew farther into the house, so it seemed, retreating behind shadows and that shemozzle in the foreground, and small boys sometimes crept up and rang the bell or threw stones on the roof. It naturally attracted attention, increasingly so, as the other houses became renovated. A sign in green biro, 'NO HAWKERS', appeared on the gate, although door-to-door salesmen, if you don't count the Mormons, haven't appeared in years and, even if they had, it's doubtful they would have called.

The various horizontal lines had filled with dirt and moved apart, no longer parallel but wandered and concentrated around the shut mouth and dull windows and, what with additional cracks and unexpected shadows, formed a network of wrinkles, a stubborn complexity. A kind of weariness grew as the house brooded, which was not obvious before. More and more it drooped. After all, he couldn't care less. It was futility. It happened gradually until one day it became clear and stayed that way. The steps, now grey, blurred into a jutting chin.

So he passed the years, inside.

Suddenly registering one morning, like the rare appearance of Parker along the footpath, was the bulge on the right-hand side, quite a rupture, a weakness there. And it's still there today. That can be a problem with the old weatherboards.

Parker put his bike away. Under the house. Not long after, he retired. That was only a few years ago.

He kept his thoughts to himself.

Dark birds as small as flies buzzed around the mouth. A blocked chimney became a recurring minor trouble and, beginning around March, the bathroom became incontinent, quite unreliable. Other gutters slipped at the side.

It settled on its shoulders, its eyes almost closed.

A vibration, a tic, developed and accelerated even in the still conditions of Brisbane. It was that loose downpipe, the skinny elbow on the right.

And now this, or at last: unknown to Parker, or to anyone else in the street, white ants had been at the insides, destroying and multiplying, attacking beneath the surfaces. Evidently it had been going on for some time. The collapse when it came was sudden and complete. It has come as a shock. For a long time, almost since the war, it seemed no one had really been living there and now there's only a house.

Huebler

Some people will go out of their way to avoid help, and I suspect Douglas Huebler falls into this class. The various 'feelers' put out to him have so far met with a stubborn silence. It seems Huebler is determined to go ahead, rushing into it, alone.

His announcement was made with appropriate fanfare on the floor of a Paris art gallery back in October, 1972.*

It was his intention, he declared, to 'photographically document... the existence of everyone alive'.

Pause. Let it sink in.

He was doing this 'to produce the most authentic representation of the human species that may be assembled'.

'Editions of the work will be periodically issued in a vari-

*Galerie Yvon Lambert.

ety of topical modes: "100,000 people", "people personally known to the artist", "look-alikes", "overlaps", etc.' Until he had photographed *everybody*.

A strange ambitious task, by any standards; and I wish him luck. He's going to need it. Sceptics have already pointed out that to photograph 'everyone alive' could wear out a dozen men, let alone one. But Huebler is adamant. He is an artist (striving after the impossible), and only in his early forties.

Personally, I find his list of the twenty-three people he intends to begin with very interesting (he wants *At least one person who is incapable of sin, At least one who may outlive art,* to mention but two). It so happens I know the whereabouts, have met in the course of my life, his twenty-three people, or 'types'. I offer them to Huebler, helping him, one artist to another, whether he likes it or not. If Huebler wants more information, such as addresses, he knows where to contact me.

1. At least one person who always has the last word.

A word first about his status, marital and so forth. Leslie Aldridge, MBE, runs a large but obscure department in Whitehall. He is a bachelor, or as a *Times* obituary will put it, if he succeeds in his ambition, a 'life-long bachelor'. He is tall, sober, well-off and immaculate; but not as urbane as one might expect. His clubs include the Reform. There he can be found most evenings chewing the steak-and-kidney pie.

History, its ramifications, has been Aldridge's passion, even more than most Englishmen, if that is at all possible. At the Foreign Office he is known for his memory of dates, especially to do with the monarchy and the European wars. Concern for details implies obstinacy—and Aldridge can be prickly, noticeably with subordinates. Lately at the office he has seemed preoccupied. His mind is wandering along somewhere else.

Aldridge approaching his sixtieth year has been struck by the fact of his own mortality. Apart from his name in old telephone directories—stored in the basement of the British Museum, admittedly—he is soon to disappear, without trace, as though he had never existed. The thought frightens him. His objective now is nothing less than to avoid anonymity.

At least his method is scholarly. Aldridge invents words. It consumes his thoughts, all his spare time. In a meeting he'll suddenly scribble on the back of an envelope. To have a word accepted into the language: it would be proof left behind of his existence.

It is said that 'astronaut' was first used by the writer Nabokov. Such an ordinary neologism would not satisfy Aldridge. He aims to have the last word—a rare honour—which has been, for many years, *Zymurgy* (practice or art of fermentation, as in wine-making, brewing, etc.).

Aldridge's words are:

Zynopic, adj. 1973. Pertaining to that type of blindness
    suffered by believers in astrology.
Zythm, n. 1974. The interval of breathing during
    sleep.
Zyvatiate, v. 1973. To sway or revolve with feet fixed to
    one spot while under the influence of alcohol.

His problem now is to get one of these into print. The publishers of the *Oxford English Dictionary* show a polite but sceptical interest. They always request sources. Leslie Aldridge is now writing letters and articles to magazines and newspapers, 'planting' the words. So far, until now, his words have been ignored.

2. At least one person who would rather be almost anyone else.

A tall order this one, Huebler; but I have an architect in Barcelona, in the suburb of Campo del Arpo. His name is Jose Rivera. Most evenings he can be seen on the Ramblas strolling with his family, wife on one arm, his son aged eleven on the other. A short man, thin legs, he has an unusually large head. He wears a coat and tie, the coat buttoned up. With each step, he makes fluttering movements with his hands, adjusting himself, so to speak. Huebler, you can't miss him.

Jose Rivera is one in the army of small architects who seem to exist in any given city. His office is above a leather shop. His staff consists of students or old men with weak eyes. They complain he looks over their shoulders, shouting suddenly. He pays a pittance. And sometimes he'll throw their work against a wall, or rip it into little pieces. In the same breath he'll pick up the phone and bend over backwards to please a client—small businessmen, usually smaller than he is. He has neither their respect nor that of his staff. He is bitter when one of them leaves.

It is not only lack of respect. Something in Rivera's manner (and face) produces distrust in people. Approaching a group outside a cafe he'll slap his hands as if it were cold. Men look away.

Rivera never seemed to notice. Putting this another way, he was a man who took no notice of his surroundings. Of his faults, he had decided long ago they were minor and anyway so enmeshed in the problems of the day as to go unnoticed. That was his opinion until a few weeks ago.

He was in a cafe one evening with his wife and son. His wife sat, half-smiling. Their son was looking around nonchalantly, arms on the table. Suddenly Rivera felt irritated. It was the boy's manner. He looked at the face intently. It was like a camera, Huebler, suddenly focusing: almost immediately Rivera wanted to escape.

It was his face. He saw his faults duplicated, smoothly growing. It was what other people must have seen. They were conspicuous: obviously father, son. For Rivera it was an intrusion; he felt like suddenly hitting his son hard across the face. He wanted to; strange, weak man. He went sullen and fiddled with a spoon.

If he could sever, disassociate. That became his immediate, hopeless wish. To be someone—almost anyone—else. Then all the signs displayed in the young face opposite could not point to him.

3. At least one person who is not afraid of life.

Strikes me this as being a bit woolly (almost unworthy of being included, Huebler). However:

Cyril Lindsay Roberts
Age: 54
Date of Birth: September 22, 1920
Status: married
Offspring: 3 daughters, 1 son
Height: 5'9"
Hair: left part; short back and sides; going grey
Eyes: brown. Wears spectacles (black-rimmed)
Teeth: false
Skin: now wrinkling
General Demeanour: grey
Other Characteristics: shy; moderation in all things;
    flat feet
Occupation: clerk, Lands Department
Passport Number: H 221668
Address: Melbourne, Australia
Further details on request

4. At least one person who may outlive art.

For sheer ruthlessness, surely nothing can beat the efforts of
Karl Schultz, the American 'failure'. At present he is lying in a
weakened condition in his home in Monroe, New York State.
He is forty-six, but looks about sixty.

Schultz arrived in America with his parents back in the
thirties. An early photograph shows a thin serious boy, mouth
open, and obsessive shadows like Kafka's around the eyes.
Who can know the pressures exerted by vast America on its
European immigrants? Schultz's father, a doctor, ruined his

own health building up a practice, and although he gave young Karl expensive piano lessons, and encouraged him to draw, he forced him into an American medical school. From the first day, Karl found difficulty concentrating. He was either failing or barely passing the technical exams. His friends were not the other doctors, but art students, usually with similar European backgrounds. Their large, violent canvases would soon be taking the art world by storm.

In the late forties, Schultz championed the work of those painters which then baffled, even angered, most people. He knew them all well. For example, apart from prescribing medicines at no charge, Schultz performed an abortion on a red-headed mistress of one Abstract Expressionist, who shall remain nameless, whose work hangs in every important museum in the world. Sometimes he went with them on sketching weekends, although no one took much notice of the stuff he carefully drew. Schultz was there, but on the fringe. He was never to marry. The artists' wives and girlfriends found him humourless, strange.

Schultz by then had developed a furtive manner. This along with a number of suspect cases made it difficult for him to get work, even as a relief-doctor. Several New York hospitals unaccountably struck him off their registers. Meanwhile, as the fame of his painter-friends grew, they made their excuses and saw less and less of him. His opinion of their work suddenly changed. Most people think Schultz was filled with insane jealousy at their success. Others say he genuinely found their work timid, over-decorative. The truth almost certainly lies in between.

In 1969, his father died and Schultz no longer had to

work. Shortly after, he held his first one-man show in Manhattan's most avant-garde art gallery.* At first, people thought he had met with an accident. They noticed one hand bandaged, the fingers missing. The word soon shot around. His 'work' consisted of five jars, each with a finger suspended in a clear formalin. It carried the title, FINGER PRINTS: FIVE WORKS BY KARL SCHULTZ. The exhibition notes explained how Schultz had spent 'all his life creating these works of art'. As a practising surgeon he had come to realise conventional painting could never equal the beauty, or the statement of, The Body. 'Art is usually nothing but cardboard.'

Predictably, it was denounced as a gimmick, soon to be forgotten. His former friends professed to be shocked. Only when the extent of his ambition became clear did people, the critics especially, attempt to take him seriously.

Schultz next exhibited an ear in a revolving jar. He called it VAN GOGH HERE. Most critics (subdued now) thought that was rather obvious; but it was quickly followed by his dramatic Los Angeles show—one of his legs, amputated, bent slightly at the knee, more compelling than one of Rodin's marble imitations. Other exhibitions followed. Only a few more (for reasons which must be obvious) are possible.

Schultz is in a weakened state, virtually incapacitated. Between exhibitions he has to rest for long periods and give himself sedatives. Visitors say he is remarkably clear-headed; they say he talks like a sane person. It was announced the other day his last work will consist of his suicide. An invited audience (of art lovers) and a movie camera will then watch his stubble

*The Dwan Gallery. It has since closed.

grow for five or six hours after death. The body creating after death! Hence the subtle title of this last work: STILL LIFE.

For a person to outlive art: it is a barbaric notion. Yet if there is to be a person, Karl Schultz must stand a chance. For he is preserving himself as art; and when there is no art his body, or our shocked memories of it, will remain.

5. At least one person who is pathologically modest.

There is an American industrialist (his name we all know) who has not been photographed, nor has he been seen in public, for the last. . . twenty-three years. But that doesn't help Huebler, the photographer. My 'pathologically modest' person is a woman aged about fifty-five, an American like Howard Hughes. She's easily photographed.

No one knows why Katherine White took it into her head one ordinary day back in the forties no longer to show her face to the world, to retire behind locked doors. People are quick to talk in small American towns. Miss White never married and it was loudly assumed she had been jilted again. But no one in the town had seen such a man; and no one stepped forward.

Among her friends the experienced ones thought it wise to leave her. Soon she would get over it. People would then crowd around, all solicitous; perhaps this was her melodramatic plan? Months passed. No sign from her. The postman reported her mail had dwindled to almost nothing. The front garden had become overgrown. Certain individuals prone to exaggeration swore the paint was peeling off the fence, the boards of the house. Katherine White's determination gradually dawned on the town.

Here it is interesting to note a linguistic switch. Kathy, as she was generally called, was now referred to as Katherine. And it wasn't long before this became 'Miss White'—more remote, abstract. Her friends now no longer felt sorry for her. Her behaviour seemed to insult them. She always did have airs, some recalled. Sometimes she had lapsed into cranky silences. When a group finally assembled on her porch determined to bring her to her senses, forcing entry, if necessary, they found a note on the door, unmistakably her hand:

WOULD EVERYONE LEAVE MISS WHITE ALONE

The years passed in a proliferation of undergrowth and peeling paint. Occasionally she was seen at night in the garden, or as a shadow behind the blinds. Small boys naturally hid for hours to catch a glimpse; more though left a ball if one ever landed in Miss White's tangled garden. The house was pointed out to visitors. It was perhaps inevitable her story travelled beyond the town. She had become a small legend—civic property.

In the late sixties, during the boom in colour gravure printing, a magazine from New Orleans sent out a photographer. He was an untidy young man with red hair. The mayor, for one, told him, 'If we haven't seen her face in fifteen–twenty years, son, you sure won't.'

Here then is where the 'pathology' creeps in. The photographer sent a note, and after waiting a week presented himself. A small crowd watched. The door opened. He was allowed in.

Miss White too, it seems, saw herself as an example of an Old Recluse. The photographer told of how she sat silent and trembling before the lens. She had become entwined, poor thing, in her own legend. She not only allowed herself to be photographed but continues to do so; by appointment only. Apart from the occasional eager photographer her life remains the same. She sees no one, remaining inside.

6. At least one person who is beautiful but dumb.

The sad facts are as follows:

Part of our brain is connected to the central nervous system to which examples of beauty are offered. Either they 'fit', or are rejected. With Marilyn Duncan, even women express no reservations. She should therefore be a model for neurologists. A male admirer, who happens to be her doctor, had casually pointed out her name is a combination of the two most memorable beauties of modern times.*

Yet Marilyn is unaware of her beauty. Men touching her are met with laughter, uninterest or worse, a childish tolerance. She knows nothing else! She was taken from her parents at ten and placed among lawns and silent verandahs. Compli-

*Her initials also stand for Doctor, doctor.

ments never register. She probably has no knowledge of comparisons. She was born deaf and dumb. I heard her story from the doctor. She is astonishingly beautiful, Huebler, but totally dumb. Is that what you wanted?

7. At least one person who thinks words are as concrete as objects.

Much has already been written about Zoellner in literary papers both in England and Australia. 'Zoellner's mother (whose name was also Zoellner) decided to call him Leon. His father preferred "Max", but today on the birth certificate (and other records stored in cabinets in scattered buildings) he is identified as Leon—Leon Zoellner . . .

'Whenever he thinks of the shape of himself he sees the word *Zoellner*.'

Further information recently unearthed would not go astray.

Parents were Swiss. This has been established beyond doubt. Jung mentions Zoellner's grandfather in *Memories, Dreams, Reflections*. A clue to Zoellner's thinking, perhaps it is specious, interesting though, is the news that his father was a wood carver in Berne, one who carved store names and even whole sentences for outdoor display. 1968 in England: Zoellner's wife died from a blood clot in the leg. They were out in a meadow (field or paddock) trudging. Zoellner prefers not to think about it.

Another Zoellner apart from R. L., the unrelated architect,

has appeared in the London telephone directory! She is a translator from Vienna; cold over the phone.

At 30/11/72 he was 52.7 years old. Today he has advanced to 54.2. **Age.** A period of existence. The whole or ordinary duration of life.

'Zoellner is regarded as a small person.' This still holds true. In London he moves around in a long overcoat, even in summer. A horizontal mauve scar runs across his knee, the right-hand knee; he fell down a mountain when a boy. This of course is normally invisible beneath the layer of cloth arranged in a vertical fashion (**Trousers**).

Concrete. A composition of stone-chippings, sand, gravel, pebbles, etc. formed into a mass with cement; used for foundations, pavements, etc.

His ears are larger (bulbous, bumpier too) than the ears of 30/11/72. Zoellner squeezes the lobes. How something can go on growing at his age interests him. More hair has fallen out. Muddy-grey in '72 it is silver-grey now. Weight: little changed at 113 lbs. (51.3 kilos).

Zoellner sees his name, his shape, approaching along an avenue of objects, his body consisting of parts which operate also as words. To some critics, this line of thinking—Zoellner's Definition, as it has come to be called—shows a belief in nothing. Glaring nihilism, in short. The critics of course are wrong. They should read again the carefully gathered evidence, all of it published.

Words. Verbal expression; used in a language to denote a thing, attribute or relation.

8. At least one person who may feel trapped by
   marriage.

Of all the traps, most obvious is the onomatological trap, so
obvious it is generally ignored. Onomatological? The German
poet Christien Morgenstern thought all seagulls looked as if
their names were Emma; Claudel detected a funnel and wheels
in the visual shape of the word 'locomotive'; a woman when
she marries is expected to take an alien name, grin and bear it.

Before she became a Snell, Mrs Irene Snell associated a red
dripping nose with that name, buck teeth, a sort of small-eyed
greed. It was repugnant to her, yet she fell for Brian—reliable
Brian.

Marriage bells.

There was no escaping. Envelopes arrived in the mornings
bearing the strange name. It seemed they were addressed to
another woman, one she wouldn't like. Often then she studied
her face in the mirror. She was quiet, intelligent, with no buck
teeth. But she projected her name out into the world, onto
streets and into newspapers. What would a stranger picture on
hearing her name? She found it embarrassing giving it over the
telephone.

Old Brian, busy climbing in a complex soap company,
couldn't understand it. Amazing when he arrived home the
things his wife found in him to criticise, one thing leading to
another. Then she would burst into tears. 'I still love you
though,' she'd say afterwards. Uncertain he expressed the
thought that it was time she had children. (They too would be
called Snell, she thought.)

Without driving them apart the word 'Snell' exerts its subtle pressure. It remains a yardstick for her, some would say an illogical one. It keeps interfering. Brian often finds her crabby, even with the children. This he cannot understand. They have 1) healthy children 2) nice house 3) appliances 4) big backyard 5) car, with radio and sunvisor 6) excellent prospects for further promotion. Mrs Snell will never be satisfied.

9. At least one person who cannot keep a secret.

below, two smaller holes, dark, and partially blocked as a result of a steady breeze. Dry debris visible clinging during this brief tilting. Below, wider terrain immediately widespread, a change, a sloping forest, regularly spaced, black all of it, razed regularly, adapting however to the contours. A horizontal slash there; a bright colour suddenly quarried. Its curving entrance marked by vertical scratches: emits warmth, vegetable odours. Peeling, its shape changes from ravine to skyscrapers in a blackened city beyond which is the tunnel, the void, sometimes a splashing river. Commerce is transacted. A downturn at one corner is worth closer examination. And those vertical scratches having been constantly congregated are now permanently jammed. Both the downturn and the squashing of the scratches are the inevitable result.

Ten minutes later.

A silver circle being fastened to a lobule, a slender sheet of oval calcium obscuring the view, the movements also reversed making for clumsiness, minute confusion. Perseverance prevails.

Waiting. The pinna, the meatus, the lobule are all shining. The tympanum and membrana tympani both cleaned all ready for fresh entries.

Mr and Mrs Eugene Fletcher, Apt 21B, Lincoln Towers, Cincinnati, USA.

Next!

10. At least one person whose existence is normally uneventful.

Gordon Ian Hume spends most of his time shaking his head. The place is Aberdeen's Victorian gaol. Not long ago he stepped out a free man after twenty years, but was back in a matter of days, for life. He is trying to work it out.

Local newspapers in 1952 splashed the story of the murder. Hume of course remembers it clearly. He and Neil ('Scrag') had gone out for their Friday drink together. It was late. Everyone tired. He and Neil were in their working clothes. The argument was over nothing, its origins remain obscure; but they were rolling on the floor, over bottles, cigarette butts, entwined like lovers, except for the thudding punches. In the spinning half-light a steak-knife glittered under a table. His hand found it. It touched the rising stomach. The knife went through the cotton shirt. A scream followed, then a collapsing hiss like gas escaping a moist bag. Someone's feet whispered, 'You better run. We didn't see anything.'

Hume entered the gaol wearing a beer-coloured moustache, and a narrow suit. He kept to himself. Time lost all meaning for him. The routine made the days the same. Inside the weather was the same. The faces, walls, colours, smells and men's talk were the same. The different meals seemed to distinguish the days; but, combined, their pattern made the weeks and months the same; then the years. Constant were the images of his crime, unfolding regularly, without warning, in slow motion. He came out wearing the same narrow suit, a middle-aged man with grey hair in his ears. He was ruined, displaced, forgotten.

Aberdeen's overlapping movements and noise alarmed him. Men and women displayed a careless attitude as though they were exaggerating their freedom. Hume was holding a small suitcase. To avoid pedestrians he executed a series of comical swerves, in front of women absurdly theatrical. He'd scarcely seen one in twenty years.

His first words were directed at a man smoking a strange brand of cigarettes.

'A room, if you have one.'

Apparently not loud enough.

'I would like a room, please.'

Once there Hume stretched out on the bed and trembled with confusion. The rushing sensations of Aberdeen, which resembled a violently twisted kaleidoscope, or those paintings by the Italian Futurists, were gradually interrupted by the familiar scenes from the prison, calming Hume. His spoon: yellow, sharp around the edges. He saw the ridge of dirt around the cell bars where they met the floor. The pattern of shadows across the exercise yard repeated itself. That blackhead on the warder's face—below the eye—needed squeezing. The other warder: his name he always forgot. He remembered queuing for meals and the soggy smell. The first jet airliner slowly crossed overhead, all men looking up. There was the barren arrangement of his cell, empty corridors, echoes. Prison architecture consists almost entirely of straight lines.

In the morning he ventured out, more relaxed. He passed new buildings and failed to recognise old buildings. He seemed to be approaching his old neighbourhood. Rubbing his hands he anticipated the pleasure of ordering a meal he hadn't tasted for twenty years. They rarely served a good steak in prison.

The pub was familiar, although its name was not. He chose the table with uneven legs near the door. He was taking his first sip from a pint of beer when a man came through the door. The way others greeted him showed he was a regular customer.

Hume lowered his glass. He went up to the bar. He listened carefully before touching him.

'Neil Macdonald?' he murmured. 'Scrag?'

Macdonald turned around. His face had filled out. His hair was no longer dark.

Macdonald's body arched back in surprise, wrenched by the hair, his hands clutching the air for balance. He fell to the floor, Hume on top. Hume broke a bottle. He stabbed and stabbed again at the face. The bulging throat burst. Macdonald's body subsided, became smaller. They lifted him off. Hume was sobbing, already shaking his head. Images of the prison returned, repeating themselves.

11. At least one person who is always the life of the party.

Bob Knudsen was born in 1924 at Denver, Col., the son of an Irish mother and half-German father. He made little impression at school, was rejected by the US Army when America entered the Second World War, but became a pilot in the Canadian Flying Corps. After the war he attended the University of California for a time and then led a roving life, becoming in turn a ranch hand, fruit-picker, dish-washer, lumberjack, signwriter, nightclub waiter, and car-park attendant. In 1952, the year of his marriage, he took a job as a coal-heaver at his local power station and wrote *The Power and the Pain* (1953) between the hours of midnight and 4 am. *The Big Hate* followed in 1955. He now lives on the outskirts of Toronto with his wife, five children and 'two guitars'. He lists his other interests as sky-diving, photography and local politics.

12. At least one person who is not afraid of death.

Here we have an 'overlap'. The person carefully detailed in (3) as one 'not afraid of life' is also not afraid of death. See also persons (6), (7), (8). Surprising, Huebler, the number of people not afraid of death.

Frank Carpenter should be called Graves, he is a clumsy as hell. Certainly, everything happens to *him*. At the point where the lines of chance intersect Carpenter is usually standing, or about to place his foot fatally forward. That he had learned to steer clear of ladders has not prevented him from spilling liquids; clutching at eggs; burning fingers on handles; relying on rotten gutters or hollow tree-branches; falling off logs. His movements cause alarm and laughter among others. His large slow hands. The elongated shoes. He collides with head-waiters and cyclists. Treads on his wife's flowers. Replacing a glass he'll miss the table's edge by a good two inches. As a boy his nose used to bleed. Now it perpetually leaks, apparently draining him of vital co-ordinating fluids.

Graves is cheerful and enjoys reasonable health. His body has so much iron it demagnetises clocks, compasses and gramophones. He is one of those who activate faulty lampshades; then tripping over the cord he'll turn, full of apologies.

Wales. (U.K.)

13. At least one person who manages to imagine another in the place of his, or her, lover.

I tore this out of the London *Times* on June 16, 1973. It can be reprinted here without changing a word.

Dubai, June 15. —An Englishman rescued from the Atlantic off West Africa told reporters today of how he jumped from a ship into the ocean after thinking he saw his dead wife in the water.

Mr Lawrence John Ellis, aged 31, said he stowed away in a container ship at Liverpool with a friend on May 15 because he was anxious to get to Australia where his wife had died last December.

He and his companion were allowed to work in the ship after being discovered, but he 'became very depressed' thinking about his wife.

'Nothing could stop me remembering my wife that night of May 21 ... As I walked on deck I believed I could see her in the water beckoning to me ... So certain was I that I got two lifebelts, lashed them together, and dived into the sea. I quickly surfaced and began to search for my wife. The water was ice-cold and I saw the lights of the ship disappearing.'

Mr Ellis said that with the coming of the dawn and the sun he thought he was going to die.

Badly sunburned he was about to give up hope of rescue but he saw one or two ships and waved. They did not see him so he decided to strike out for the shore. He was 100 miles off the coast of Guinea.

Finally, after 10 hours in the water, he was seen and picked up by the Italian tanker Esso Augusta.

The captain was not allowed to put the rescued man ashore at Cape Town so he arranged for him to be transferred to a supply boat at Dubai where Mr Ellis stepped ashore today. —Reuters.

14. At least one person who had achieved
    purposelessness.

One man, a gentleman in Straubing, West Germany, is spending his fortune in an attempt to re-create Ludwig II of Bavaria's artificial forest, complete with the mechanical animals, artificial whistling, the whirrings and arboreal crunchings; another (recently retired) man (white-haired) in Bairnsdale, Victoria, is devoting his remaining days to removing the weeds from the silent rows of his local *Pinus radiata* forest; a fire-watcher with blue eyes in Ontario, in what is claimed to be that country's largest commercial forest, has stood in a silver tower for thirty-four years, every day just about, binoculars handy, thermos of coffee, packed lunch, connected to the outside world by field telephone, without once seeing smoke; an old woman dying in Munich has a ladder hanging over her bed; while in London, in Battersea, two men living in the same street (Dagnell St) are trying to assemble the definitive collection of matchbox labels, and they have some beauties, though each is unaware of the other's existence.

15. At least one person who is convinced his or
    her experiences would make an interesting
    nov—

CAMOUFLAGE

16. At least one person who wants to be liked by everyone.

His employer said, 'He is a conscientious worker who doesn't call me George all the time like the others. I like that. In this business you get sick of the familiarity which I tell you is a load of bullshit. He knows too I won't have the radio on in the afternoons, he'll accept that, while the others kick up a fuss. Some nights he'll help me sweep up afterwards and ask about the kids and so forth. He's made some suggestions for the shop, some viable, like displaying the combs and blades near the cash register, though I can't say yet I've noticed the difference in the till.'

His postman said, 'That Mr Johnson knows about pigeons. He never forgets. He told me he used to keep pigeons once. They were Blue-beaks.'

A customer said, 'Where he gets his information from God knows. The one he gave for the three-fifteen came in. He knows the names and weights backwards. Maybe he reads the newspapers or he was a jockey once. Nice little feller.'

His waitress said, 'Oh, he's nice. We even know his name: Mr Johnson! He always says a word and leaves something behind.'

The second hairdresser said, 'Old George, he turns off the transistor after lunch and Gordo turns to us, "Now I'm on, boys," he says. "What'll it be? 'Dr Zhivago'? 'Strangers in the Night'?" He'll whistle all afternoon, if necessary. He can even do a good "Black and White Rag". Like all of us he hates the work and old George, and wants to get out. We've talked about opening our own shop.'

Another customer, 'Nice little feller.'

A neighbour said, 'Gordon Johnson opposite: we'd only recently moved in and he gave me a bag of fertiliser. He must have seen me putting in the vegetables. Can't say I really know him exactly, even though we're on quite a friendly first-name basis.'

His daughter said, 'I don't know, I just feel I can talk to him more. He's a million times better than her. When she starts getting on my back I go straight to him. Sometimes I have to meet him at the corner to get in first, before she sticks her claws in. He makes jokes about her to me. If I want any-thing—money, or anything—I ask him, not her.'

His wife said, 'Gordon doesn't say much now. I can see he's listening though. I tell him everything, oh yes. I look for-ward to him arriving home. When he's around it's better, nat-urally. I say, though, he doesn't talk much, but I suppose I like that in a man; a quiet one.'

17. At least one person whose existence was
    foreordained.

In an old country where the physiognomics have long ago been settled people take their faces for granted. Young coun-tries are perhaps not so lucky. The Australian Face, even the American Face, is not finished yet. In Australia the signs are the jaw and large ears will become characteristic, but what are they—a mere two hundred years old? Interesting how speech patterns evolve faster: but that's another story.

The example here of a person 'whose existence was fore-ordained' could only come from an old country. Here, it is Italy.

Others have surely noticed her in Verona. She has a small vegetable stall in the main market. While the other women screech out their bargains she only smiles slightly. She is a woman of simple, arresting beauty. This woman—her face, shoulders, folded hands—first appeared during the Renaissance. Then, she was the wife of one Francesco de Giocondo. Leonardo painted her portrait. Now she has appeared again. Not reincarnated, but repeated by an overlap of Italian genetics. Italy is old enough.

Her face is surrounded by an oval of darkness. It's her hair curving down merging with a blouse of similar colour. Attention is drawn naturally within to her skin, the puffy curves which almost make her voluptuous, yet not quite. Some hesitancy hovers in her eyes. She is still young. Vasari in his over-rated *Lives* writes that Leonardo employed musicians and jesters 'to keep her full of merriment and so chase away the melancholy that painters usually give to a portrait'. This is nonsense. In the market in Verona she holds that smile all day without artificial assistance. Where she differs from Leonardo's portrait is her name, which begins with a different letter, and her folded hands—on her marriage finger she has a thick gold ring.

And this.

Close up, as one occasionally sees in young northern Italian women, she has the beginnings of a small moustache. With her though it was perhaps inevitable. Marcel Duchamp painted one on in the year 1919.

18. At least one person who hears voices.

Yes, Joan has been hearing voices on and off for seven years now. She is a switchboard operator. The clamps of spring-steel they use in the Edinburgh Exchange are an ancient design, squashing the ears, which is probably why Joan has sensible hair, never permed, short like a boy's. What was that, Huebler? The girls get along fine, she's popular, chattering between calls. There are several avenues of girls, pulling out wires, constantly changing a pattern, hypnotic to watch, a strange job to have when you think about it, though it can't be as bad as Persian carpet-weaving, which has a similar appearance. Joan met her husband, if met is the right word, through her job: a maroon wire plugged in and there was his voice. She was on night shift. Of course, you get a lot of lewd bravado on the part of men who have nothing better to do, especially at night, than ring up for a joke, on the off chance of . . . you know what. Depends entirely on the mood of the girls. His voice was deep, easy, and made her laugh. I think you've been drinking. Tell me the colour of your hair, he replied. It was a fine answer on his part. In her job she often wondered what a particular voice looked like. Just a minute—she had other calls. I think I've got her, he winked at the boys, all of them jammed in the telephone booth. But it was raining. They met the following night. (She wanted to make sure anyway.)

His voice had been deep and confident, yet she saw a thin small man, plainly nervous; he was alone. He stepped off a 350cc AJS single, coil front springs, brass Amal carburettor (another old design). One shoelace was undone. He was a bookie's assistant, soon to lose his job. Car's getting fixed, he explained, nodding to the leaking motorbike. She was to discover later he didn't have a car. Odd then that it should continue, she efficient, sensible, the clear voice over the telephone, while he, never mind his name, specialised in the narrowly missed opportunity, always, and yet a boastful casualness; she spent two years on and off the AJS, sitting in his pubs with his male friends who ignored her. She married him. Takes all types.

The other girls who had shaken their heads all along nod their heads in unison, vindicated. He has left her. Of course. All right. These things happen. Joan is back where she started, hearing voices. She has a son, his, and has to avoid the night shift.

19. At least one person totally without charisma.

He can be seen between the hours of 9.30 and 12.30 and, after lunch, 2.30 and 5.30. Go down Firestone Boulevard, Los Angeles. Cross the lights near the Gulf pumps. On the left is a men's store. Stand before the window. Watch: eventually a window mannequin will move slightly. Usually the elbow of an outstretched arm growing tired, or the fixed smile. This is George Ellison, a human dummy. Good God! What is the world coming to?

Little is known about Ellison. At home he has a daughter and son. The son, about to enter college, answers him back.

I suggest you use a tripod for this one, Huebler, but you're the expert. I don't know how Ellison is going to react with you taking his picture there. The manager says he has had the job for eleven months. The brainwave was his (the manager's) to put a living person in the window. But even to discuss the subject seemed to throw the manager into a curt mood. Ellison is doing the job so exactly it is hard to distinguish him from the real mannequins. How he'll even show in a photograph, Huebler, I don't know.

20. At least one person who is poor but happy.

Of course the word 'poor' is relative.

An uncle of mine, a relative, laughs at everything I say and hasn't got a bean. I think he owes money. 'To hell with the expense, give the canary another seed' is one of his mottoes, if not his philosophy. 'My philanthropy,' he argues. He laughs. I laugh. He's always making weak jokes like that. 'Seeing you're travelling on the *Titanic*, why go steerage?' Good question. The rest of the family doesn't laugh. He wears sandals, open-necked shirts. For several years he lived in a garage and later on the edge of town in a shack made from kero tins. He doesn't feel the cold. 'You should be on the stage,' he says to my father, a solemn opposite, 'the next one leaves in five minutes. Don't miss it.' Even my mother laughed. All this shows that my uncle is happy.

He was never on stage, though he regularly mentions a friend who was. It was a balancing act which depended on centrifugal force. The friend would swing a bowl of goldfish around his head without spilling a drop. The RSPCA complained and he then changed to carrots. My uncle argued that fish in a bowl could only swim in circles anyway. He once passed a multi-millionaire being assisted into his limousine by the chauffeur, and cried out, 'Good evening, sir. It must be such a helluva burden. Can you spare a shilling?' Normally he never discussed anything serious.

Yet he will discuss anything! He is loved by door-to-door salesmen, hitch-hikers, barmen, moneylenders, tourists and women. He has strong red health. That helps. He said it was because he has never read newspapers.

I mentioned women. There's a funny thing. For all his obvious popularity with them in the short term he has subsequent trouble over the long haul. My uncle has been three times divorced. A fourth woman, who would have been another wife, he lost in a motor accident. 'Fourth time is lucky,' he says, making us laugh. At this my mother scarcely smiles. Women like him and give him money, yet they continue to leave. Still, that's not our business. My poor uncle will be happy to be photographed.

21. At least one person who is incapable of sin.

Here are two, a brother and sister. They share a house in Belfast, a stone's throw, no less, from the Falls Road. Wall to wall, all similar, the houses share the same roofline. It can be a snake in the mist. Net curtains preserve their secrets. The brother and sister have the wallpaper left by their parents, smelling of moisture and peeling, the original colour shown by a bright cross-shape around an old nail. They were born in poverty, and although almost fifty they sleep together in the one bed, a habit beginning in childhood and allowed to continue into their teens, their parents dying within a year of each other. They wear flannel nightwear, although by early morning her gown is sometimes above her head.

The brother is a large slow man with fat hands. He has blue eyes. He goes off early to work in the Harland and Wolff shipyards, a welder, known to be harmless, a Catholic among nine thousand, mainly Protestants. They leave him alone. When one of them begins a dirty story he moves away. For lunch he has white sandwiches, cut by his sister.

She works in a drapery store not far away. Finishing early he sometimes goes in to surprise her, not having much else to do. She has a small face. Her eyes, darker than his, are slightly too close together: enough to be noticeable. In the Bogside pubs she is known for her unpredictable temper.

She is more religious than her brother. At Easter last year she left something in a shopping bag which took away the face of a British soldier poking at it with a pole. Murderer, then. She has stolen in her time and told countless lies. She blasphemes. What else: illicit love with married men, more than once, though not recently. Yet she is incapable of sin. She has yet to commit it.

In bed she has allowed her brother to study her swelling breasts, she lying back on the bed, her hand stroking his neck. It began recently. The nipples have been abruptly fumbled, licked. Her brother is all trembles, wide-eyed, while she measures her own spreading gentleness. Just as naturally, it seems, his knee pushed open her legs. He has rolled on top of her. There they have stopped.

Anthropologists are agreed. They know of no culture which does not contain a single forbidden act, the ultimate sin.

All other 'sins' are perhaps permissible—words attached to a religion. So far, the brother and sister have drawn back, knowingly. But there is, according to the Book of Ecclesiastes, a time for all things. Amen. Hurry to Belfast, Huebler.

22. At least one person whose unique sexual capacities have no outlet.

Mrs Cartwright has lived in India for most of her life, and I met her beside the swimming pool at the Breach Candy Club, Bombay. This was in 1968. It was a Sunday morning; very, very humid. I was new to India. The Shiv Sena had rioted during the week. Cars were overturned, shops, buses and taxis burnt. Over a hundred were rumoured dead. The curfew lifted only that morning allowed us, the European community, to get together, and I was naturally eager to hear the Old Hands, including Mrs Cartwright's husband, arguing in the deckchairs on my right; but no, Mrs Cartwright had her hand on my arm discussing something altogether different, unimportant. When she opened her handbag and took out a photograph I realised the subject had been herself.

'What is this?' I said, and glanced back. Any chance of joining them was rapidly disappearing.

'I had a figure then,' she said in a tone without apparent interest, 'as good as anything you see here.'

We all know how the tropics accelerate the ageing process. It was brought home to me by Mrs Cartwright's thumb which held the photograph. Soaked in suntan oil it was a mass of overlapping circles, expansions and contractions. The nail was painted red. Then the photograph. I found myself leaning forward. It was her on a cane couch, unmarried, before the war. 'I was twenty-three, sweet and innocent.' Adding, 'I gave Frank a merry chase.'

She lay there in a blouse half-undone and wide trousers. She had a wide-apart face like a generous country.

Perspiration skidded down my back. It must have been the humidity. Feeling her watching I nodded once again at the photograph.

This released more words.

'Parties, weekends, every night. The life has left India.'

'What happened during the war?' I asked, bringing the subject more or less back to the Old Hands. All I could see of Frank Cartwright was his broad Englishman's back.

'We were married before it. I sat around waiting for Frank in Ceylon. Ceylon was full of American boys.'

Careless, she blew smoke in my face. Suddenly she began laughing at something, her wrinkles shaking.

'Wasn't I a beauty?' she said, taking the photograph back. Before I could answer, she went on, 'Now I'll show you something else. This is the oddest thing that ever happened to me.' Laughing still, she dug around in the handbag. Suddenly she stopped. 'But you don't go telling anyone. I haven't shown this to a soul. Not even Frank.'

Frank holding court had his back to us.

She inhaled her cigarette and produced another photograph.

'This is me. Don't blush.'

I let out a slow whistle.

It was another prewar pose, this time nude. She lay on cushions. Her hair was down. She had a large smiling mouth.

Mrs Cartwright gave a hoarse, slightly embarrassed laugh.

'Ver-eee nice,' I said, studying her body professionally, but gradually reddening. Then, 'Aye, this is a painting!'

'Now I'll tell you,' she said.

'When we married, Frank and I moved into his place in Delhi. Frank was already in the army, playing soldiers. Next door was an artist—I forget his name—a nice Bengali boy. I used to go in during the day. He was always polite. He used to listen to me.' She lit another cigarette. I held on to the photograph. 'I think he may have loved me,' she said, blowing smoke, 'but even after I was married I had men running after me. I could see he wouldn't touch me—the Bengali—and one afternoon, it was one of those terrible hot Delhi days, I threw off my clothes. "Paint me!" I said. Everything then was so bloody quiet there.'

The Bombay crows were crying. I felt India's heat drying my throat.

'The poor boy was shocked. He lost his tongue. But he began painting. The next day he brought the cushions you see there. And I enjoyed it! Lying back on the cushions.'

'How long did he take?' I asked, studying the painting.

'Five weeks. It was finished the morning war was declared. I remember thinking that the nations were fighting over the qualities of my body.'

Again she laughed. She stubbed out her cigarette.

'Anyway, Frank ran off to fight. I spent five years vegetating in Ceylon. Look at me now! In 1946, we went back to

Delhi. Frank still had another year in the army. A cheeky young sergeant showed us our married quarters; he kept brushing past me in the doorways. Then—and I nearly died—someone took us into the officers' mess. Hanging over the fireplace was the oil painting, me with my titties exposed. I stood stock still, waiting for one of them to recognise me. But no one did. Not even Frank!' Mrs Cartwright paused. 'But then he's as blind as a bat.'

'It's still up there,' she added, taking the photograph back from me, 'I saw it only the other day.'

She put it back in the envelope, closing her ridiculous handbag. She sighed and looked around the pool. 'All those dirty old men, licking their chops over me.'

23. At least one person for whom reality is richer than the artist's fantasies.

Huebler, are you American? Hue-bler: sounds it. Could be. Your ancestors perhaps were European originally. Are you married? Happy? Any children? Perhaps not married. Or no longer. I understand. To return to your ancestors: mother and father still around? Good health? No problems, economic or otherwise? These are troubled times. Myself, I have lost a parent. No good, Huebler! You're stubborn, do you know that?

Nice weather today. Little cold this morning giving way to intermittent sunshine. Outside, figures move forward, some in heavy coats: I'd say they've underestimated the temperature. Walking along a path put down for them, a strip set aside, amazing vertical action. Wood grain! I don't suppose you've

had a chance to study it lately. Wood grain on this desk is infi-
nite, Huebler, eddying flatly under the pad—I'm lifting the
pad—like giant thumb prints, harmless isobars even.

Huebler. Sounds American. What do you look like? I
mean, how would you describe yourself? Do you stand out in
a crowd? An ambitious visionary tends to. Tell me! Tall? Compelling features in ill-fitting clothes? How long have you been
taking photographs? Not tall: bow-legged? Strong calves for
certain. You'll need energy, Huebler. What sort of camera? Ko-
dak film? You have a pimple or two between your shoulder-
blades where your hand can't reach. Troubling you, Huebler?
Tiredness is oppressive. Has your watchstrap left a mark on
your wrist? Where do you live exactly? Rented accommodation? Tell me the city! Blue eyes? Huebler, are you circum-
cised? A detail, I know, but interesting to some nevertheless.
Why are you doing this? I have been thinking. Huebler. I
think we all have been.

Camouflage

All things considered, piano-tuning is a harmless profession. Working by themselves in rooms filled with other people's most intimate belongings, piano-tuners give the impression of wanting to be somewhere else. They're known to jump at unexpected sounds. At the sight of blood they'd run a mile. And yet early in 1943 Eric Banerjee, along with some other able-bodied men, was called up by the army to defend his country. 'Mr Banerjee wouldn't hurt a fly'—that came from a widow who lived alone in the Adelaide foothills, where her Beale piano kept going out of tune.

It followed that, if a man as harmless as Eric Banerjee had been called up, the situation to the north was far more serious than the authorities were letting on.

For the piano-tuner it could not have come at a worse time. He had a wife, whose name was Lina, and a daughter who was just beginning to talk. It had taken him years to build up a client base, which barely gave them enough to live on. Then almost overnight—when the war broke out—there was a simultaneous lifting of piano lids across the suburbs of Adelaide, and suddenly Banerjee found he couldn't keep up with demand. These were solid inquiries from piano owners he had never heard of before, in suburbs such as Norwood and St Peters, even as far away as Hackney. In times of uncertainty people turn for consolation to music. Apparently the same thing happened in London, Berlin, Leningrad.

'I'd say it was some sort of clerical mistake.' He patted his wife on the shoulder. 'I won't be gone for long.' She'd burst into hysterical sobbing. What would happen now to her and their baby daughter?

Already the city was half empty. Every day the newspapers carried grainy photographs of another explosion or oil refinery in flames, another ship going down and, if that wasn't alarming enough, maps of Burma and Singapore which had thick black arrows sprouting from the Japanese army, all curving south in an accelerating mass, not only towards Australia basking in the Pacific, but heading for Adelaide, its streets wide open, defenceless. And now it was as if he, and he alone, had been selected to single-handedly stand in front and stop the advancing horde.

This uncertainty and the vague fear that he might be killed gradually gave way to a curiosity at leaving home and his wife and child, although he was bound in strong intimacy to them, and entering—embarking upon—a series of situations on a large scale, in the company of other men.

Besides, there was little he could do. The immediate future

was out of his hands; he could feel himself carried along by altogether larger forces, a small body in a larger mass, which was a pleasant feeling too.

Eric Banerjee gave his date of birth and next of kin, and was examined by a doctor. Later he was handed a small piece of paper to exchange for a uniform the colour of fresh cow manure, and a pair of stiff black boots with leather laces. At home he put the uniform on again and gave his wife in the kitchen a snappy salute.

It was so unusual she began shouting. 'And now look what you've done!' Their daughter was pointing at him, screwing her face, and crying.

On the last morning Banerjee finished shaving and looked at himself in the mirror.

He tried to imagine what other people would make of his face, especially the many different strangers he was about to meet. In the mirror he couldn't get a clear impression of himself. He tried an earnest look, a canny one, then out-and-out gloom and pessimism, all with the help of the uniform. He didn't bother trying to look fierce. For a moment he wondered how he looked to others—older or younger? He then returned to normal, or what appeared to be normal—he still seemed to be pulling faces.

'I'll be off then,' he said to Lina. 'I can't exactly say, of course, when I'll be back.'

He heard his voice, solemn and stiff, as if these were to be the last words to his wife.

'You're not even sorry you're going,' she had cried the night before.

Now at the moment of departure something already felt missing. At the same time, everything around him—including himself—felt too ordinary. Surely at a moment like this everything should have been different. Turning, he kept giving little waves with his pianist's fingers. Already he was almost having a good time.

At the barracks he was told to stand to attention out in the sun with some other men. Later there was a second, more leisurely inspection where he had to stand in a line, naked. Then an exceptionally thin officer seated at a trestle table, whom Banerjee recognised as his local bank manager, asked some brief questions.

Banerjee's qualifications were not impressive. The officer sighed, as if the war was now well and truly lost, and taking a match winced as he dug around inside his ear. With some disappointment Banerjee thought he might be let off—sent home. But the officer reached for a rubber stamp. Because of his occupation, 'piano-tuner', Banerjee was placed with a small group in the shade, to one side. These were artists, as well as a lecturer in English who sat on the ground clasping his knees, a picture-framer, a librarian as deaf as a post, a signwriter who did shop windows, and others too overweight or too something to hold a rifle.

Over the next few days they marched backwards and forwards, working on drill. They were shown how to look after equipment and when to salute. Nothing much more.

A week had barely gone by when the order came to report to the railway station, immediately. It was late afternoon. Lugging their gear they sauntered behind a silver-haired man who appeared to be a leader. As Banerjee hummed a tune he wondered if they should have been in step. From a passing truck soldiers whistled and laughed at them.

'I don't have a clue where we're heading.'

'Search me,' said the signwriter.

Banerjee took a cigarette offered, though he never really smoked.

Every seat was taken with soldiers. Most were young, barely twenty, but actually looked like soldiers. Tanned, tired-looking faces in worn uniforms. They played cards or sprawled about in greatcoats. A few gazed out the window, even after it was dark. A few tried writing letters. Some shouted out in their sleep. The motion of the long train and the absence of a known destination gave the impression they were travelling endlessly, while at the same time remaining in the one spot. To Banerjee, the feeling of leaving an old life and heading towards a new unknown life became blurry. A voice asked, 'What day are we?' Later another, 'Has anyone got the time?'

All that night, the following day and the next they travelled slowly, with frequent stops, up the centre of Australia. They were heading towards the fighting. The further north they went the more they stopped in daylight, waiting for hours on end. On the third day the train remained motionless all afternoon, creaking in the heat, and they saw nothing through the windows but low grey bush, a few worn hills in the distance.

A young soldier spoke for the first time. 'As far as I'm concerned the Japs can have it.'

The horizon remained. Nothing moved. And the low horizon may have spread the melancholy among them. Banerjee tried to picture his street, his front fence and house, the appearance of his wife. Their daughter was growing up while he waited in the train. The other men had fallen silent, some nodding off.

The train stopped. It creaked forward, stopped again. In the dark a sergeant came through, shouting his head off.

It was Banerjee's group which was told to fall in outside.

The cold and unevenness of the ground alongside the train had them stumbling and swearing. They herded together, hands in greatcoats, and waited.

'Put out that cigarette!'—meaning the light receding.

Banerjee didn't even smile. After it could no longer be seen the train could still be heard; but what remained was soon enough replaced by the immense silence. To clear a throat out there would be deafening, worse than a concert hall.

Banerjee was probably the first to pick up the sound, a smaller engine. Another ten minutes must have passed before the truck stopped before them, tall and vibrating. It took some trouble climbing into the back. They sat facing each other under a tarpaulin roof; and the truck turned, climbing over bushes, and made its way back along the same track, over low bush and rocks, and what appeared to be creek beds, pale stones there, while the dust funnelled out behind them, obliterating the stars.

After two hours of this—bumping about, grabbing at arms, crashing of gears—the truck slowed, the path became smoother.

Someone nudged, 'Stick your head out and see where we are.'

To no one in particular Banerjee said, 'I've never been in this part of the world before.'

Leaning forward he saw a large silver shed and other buildings in the moonlight.

They were shown into a long hut. Banerjee lay down in his uniform and slept.

At first light the desolate composition of the aerodrome was revealed. A runway had been cut into the mulga by a team of crack Americans. Here then were the nation's forward defences. And not a cloud in the sky. Already it was warm. Everything spanking new in the morning light. There were two large hangars, sheds and a long water tank. Down the far end were smaller buildings and men moving about.

A man wearing an officer's cap and khaki shorts stood before them. Eric could have sworn he used to see him at the recitals at the Town Hall, although there he wore a beard.

Clearing his throat he spoke casually, but firmly. He didn't expect much in the way of formality, he said. He did however expect their full attention. 'It would make our job a darned sight easier.' The enemy, he explained, was not far away and coming closer 'as we speak'. The aerodrome was one of a number along the top of the Northern Territory. Their task was to paint—every inch of the place. 'At the moment it is a sitting duck,' was how he put it. The slightest patch of bare metal, he explained, could flash a signal to the enemy in the sky. To demonstrate he fished around in a pocket and held up a three-pence—'like so'.

The camouflage officer then squinted at the new roofs shining in the sun. 'The art in all this is deception,' he said thoughtfully, as if the whole thing was a game. He spoke of the 'science of appearances', of fooling the oriental eye. It was a matter of applying the right colours in certain combinations and patterns.

Banerjee was handed a bucket of ochre paint, a wide brush, and assigned the roof of the main hangar. It took a while to get used to the height. And the roof itself was slippery. Close up it didn't seem possible that his hand, which produced a strip of rapidly drying colour, would make any difference to the larger situation, the advance of mechanised armies across islands and continents. Further along other men were slapping on industrial grey.

As the day progressed the huge expanse of corrugated iron warmed up, almost too hot to touch, and glittered more, straining the eyes.

The others had taken off their shirts and the signwriter nearby knotted his handkerchief at the corners and put it on his head. Now and then the officer in shorts appeared below and studied their progress through the reverse end of binoculars. Pointing with a long stick he shouted up to Banerjee to give more curve there to the red ochre. He made a parallel flowing movement with his hands. 'Like a woman's hips. Think of her hips!' which allowed Banerjee in unpromising surroundings to wander over the softness of his wife's body— at that moment probably bent over their daughter. 'That's good, a little more to the left. Good man,' the voice continued.

At the morning tea-break Banerjee sat in the shade and closed his eyes.

The Americans were recognisable by their sunglasses. When he returned their greetings Banerjee thought everybody could do with sunglasses up on the roof.

And this thought made him realise he was doing his best, and he felt satisfied.

Piano-tuning hadn't been his first choice of profession. When Eric was about ten the *News* ran a photo of him seated at the Town Hall's Steinway, his feet barely touching the pedals, reeling off a mazurka by Chopin he had sighted only minutes before. That tabloid which always had a reputation in Adelaide for fearlessness came out and announced 'our latest prodigy'. A career in the concert hall beckoned. Accordingly his normal schooling was adjusted and his parents made the necessary sacrifices, going without small luxuries, such as extra clothes or holidays. The teacher appointed was considered one of the best available: Viennese, arthritic, cameo brooch.

Banerjee became accustomed to applause. His combed hair, jug ears. He hardly ever missed a note. As he went on playing here and there, as it all flowed more like water out of his hands, years passed, and he began to wonder, as did others, whether his playing was progressing. Flaws in his technique began to show. These were probably flaws in temperament; he didn't seem conscious of them. He was taller and heavier than most pianists.

By his mid-twenties Eric Banerjee had given very few recitals, at least not in the main venues. However hard he worked the world around him remained just out of reach. It was as if a steady invisible force held him in the one spot, and now began pushing him back slightly and to one side. Almost without noticing he was playing more and more at less demanding venues, weddings, church gatherings, schools and the like, and didn't seem to mind. He felt comfortable there. Both parents died. He hardly ever attended a concert. In the space of a few more years he retreated still further until, after taking in a few pupils, which is how he met his wife, he came to rest, it would appear, piano-tuning, which may be some distance from bowing in tails on the concert platform, but is in the general vicinity, and supplied a small, regular income.

For all this, Banerjee had escaped the bitterness endemic among piano-tuners. He was pale and had a small valley in his chin. One advantage of his profession was that it left his head permanently inclined to one side, which gave the impression he was a good listener.

Banerjee was close to forty. Looking back he wondered where it had all gone. What happened in all those years? Most people didn't know or care if a piano was out of tune; only a few could tell the difference. And yet there he would surely be, continuing into the sunset, crossing from one manganese brick house to the next, one suburb to another, adjusting the progressions of sound plucked out of the air, as it were. If anyone could understand it would be the officer who spoke of 'deception'. On the street between the dusty box hedges time it-self seemed to have slowed to a crawl. Any sign of life was at mid-distance; and all so quiet it was as if he was going deaf.

Not that he wanted disturbance, disruption, surprise and so on. A certain order was necessary in his line of work. These thoughts he kept to himself. Yet increasingly he felt a dissatis-faction, as though he had all along been avoiding something which was actually closer to the true surface of life.

By early afternoon the officer had taken pity on them. The academic had lost his glasses. Further along another man was silently vomiting; Banerjee too felt dizzy—headache behind the eyes. There was paint on his fingers, elbows and wrists. Perspiration had also mixed with reddish dust and muck. The golden rule in his profession: clean fingernails. Now look at them. The one remaining sign of his previous life was the vi-bration in one leg, and he tried shifting his weight, for of course it reminded him of the final tremor of a tuning fork.

As they made their way down, Banerjee lost control of the bucket and paint ran all over his pattern.

'Leave it till morning,' the officer said. 'If the Japs come over we're done for anyway.'

'These blisters, I couldn't grip.'

'I take it you don't, as a rule, work with your hands.'

Banerjee was examining his palm. 'Piano.' He looked up. 'I mean piano-tuner, that's what I do.'

All he wanted just then was to drink a gallon of water, and shut his eyes to the light, which he did with the help of an elbow, only to see the roof in all its glittering endlessness. He didn't feel like eating.

But it only took a few days for his body to grow into the work. His hands soon enough hardened. With his shirt off and sun on his back he became absorbed in the task. The undulating pattern of red-grey was interesting in itself; the idea behind it made them merry.

A rivalry began with the men on the other roof to see who could finish first. These men Banerjee knew from the dormitory. In ordinary life some were successful painters of hills and trees—Horace, Arthur, Russell were names Banerjee heard. The picture-framer was apparently known to them. He suggested the artists sign each sheet of iron when they finished. The man with prematurely white eyebrows nodded. 'That's the only way you'll make a killing.'

Banerjee enjoyed this sort of banter, even if he was on the fringe. There was not much of it in the day of a piano-turner; and it would never occur to him to banter with his wife Lina, who had anyway become curiously solemn after having their child.

Early one afternoon planes were spotted—three of them, high. Leaning back they shielded their eyes to watch. The officer on the ground had to clap and yell to get them down—'For Christ sake!'—off the roof.

Later that same day they had a grandstand view of the first two planes to land.

And just when the dust had settled, and they were admiring the practised efficiency of the Americans parking the planes, they ran out of paint. There was nothing to do but come down on ladders and sit around in the shade, where it was still hot.

Without effort, Banerjee was a man who kept his thoughts to himself; preferred to stay back than join in. Yet there he was more or less part of the group mumbling and wisecracking. Often they were joined by the camouflage officer. After all, he had nothing much to do either. Close up Banerjee noticed his face was infested with small lines.

The officer looked up from scratching the ground with his stick. 'I don't know what's happened to our paint.' To Banerjee he added, 'In war there's more waiting than shooting. Always was.' When the talk turned to music Banerjee could have said something, and with real authority; instead he listened while letting his thoughts wander among other things.

On the third or fourth day one of the pilots squatted beside him. After talking about his hometown (St Louis) and his parents, he held out a hand and introduced himself.

Banerjee married late. Lina was barely twenty-one. He had taken her away from everybody else; that was how it later felt. All her privacies she transferred to him. The way their habits became one she accepted with busy contentment; while Banerjee composed his face, unable to find his natural state.

He was strong all right, in the sense that he practised a certain distance, the same way he had played the piano. But Lina, she knew more; she always had. It was part of her flow, along with blood.

Whenever he paused and considered his wife he first saw her name, then found he knew very little, virtually nothing, about her; what went on in her mind, the way she came to de-cisions—no idea. He could not get a firm outline; and he knew only a little more about himself. More than anything else he was aware of her needs, and how he reacted to them. She had a slightly clipped voice.

She had gone to him for piano lessons. When he appeared he said he was no longer taking pupils. But that didn't stop her. Marriage was a continuation. Later, she explained how she'd heard him playing in the next room, and then his voice, though unable to catch his words. Without seeing him she had turned to her mother, 'That man is for me. He will do.'

'Even though you didn't hear a word I said? I was proba-bly talking nothing but rot?'

But then Lina's faith in situations invariably impressed him. She could be very solemn, sometimes. She was a woman who couldn't leave things alone; constantly rearranging things on tables, plates, sideboards. She also had a way of peeling an orange with one hand, which for some reason irritated him. Banerjee knew he should be thinking more about her, his wife; and their own daughter. She complained, as she once put it, he was 'somewhere else'. Very fond of her pale shape. Her spread-ing generosity.

One afternoon Banerjee and the picture-framer were invited by the pilot and another American for a drive to the nearest town, Katherine, about an hour away. The jeep had a white star on the bonnet; and, unusual for a pilot, he drove one-hand, crashing into bushes and rocks instead of driving around. 'Know any songs?' he called out over his shoulder.

Both Americans began singing boogie-woogie, banging on the dashboard.

They reached the town—a few bits of glittering tin.

It was here the picture-framer spoke up. 'I've got a wife called Katherine,' he said. 'She's a wonderful woman.'

Leaning over the steering wheel the driver was looking for a place to drink. 'Well, we're about to enter Katherine right now. All of us. You mind?'

The other American was smiling.

Some time later Banerjee played the piano. Nobody appeared to be listening. The flow of notes he produced seemed independent of his hands and fingers, almost as if the music played itself.

The pilot and the picture-framer beckoned from a table. Between them were two women, one an ageing redhead. Her friend, Banerjee noticed, had dirty feet.

Both women were looking up at Banerjee.

'Sit down,' the pilot pointed. 'Take the weight off those old feet.' Leaning against the redhead he said with real seriousness, 'I've got my own aeroplane back at the base.'

'That beats playing a piano. Any day,' said the younger one.

The redhead was still looking at Banerjee. 'Don't smile, it might crack your face.'

'Hey, if a plane comes over and waggles its wings, you'll know it's me.' Taking her chin in his hand, the pilot winked at Banerjee. From the bar the tubby American constantly waved, touching base.

The drinking, the reaching out for women; the congestion

of words. It was the opposite to his usual way of living. Banerjee went out and stood under the stars. He tried to think clearly. The immense calm enforced by the earth and sky, at least over this small part of it, at that moment. Also, he distinctly felt the coldness of planets.

When it was time to return he found the picture-framer squatting outside with his head in his hands. And in shadow behind the hotel he glimpsed against the wall the tall redhead holding the shoulders of one of the Americans, her pale dress above her hips.

On the way back the pilot kept driving off the track. 'I need a navigator. Where are the navigators around here?' He looked around at his friend asleep.

Seated in front Banerjee didn't know where they were. 'Keep going,' he pointed, straight ahead.

On the Thursday both hangars were finished. Everybody assembled on the ground and looked up, shielding their eyes, and were pleased with their work—about eight men, without shirts, splattered in paint. Still to be done were the long walls and ends of the buildings, the vertical surfaces. And there were sheds, the water tank, bits of equipment.

The camouflage officer unlocked one of the sheds. It was stacked with tins of beef and jam. 'Will you have a look at that? Not a bloody drop of petrol to send a plane up, but plenty of tinned peaches.'

He stood looking at it, shaking his head. He wondered if Banerjee and the picture-framer could fashion a patch of green water and a dead tree out of packing cases and sheets of tin, to be placed at one side of the runway. 'A nice touch.' Gradually the pattern was coming together.

For Banerjee these counted among his happiest days. The last time he had been as happy was when he had been ill. For days lying in bed at home, barely conscious of his surroundings; it was as if the walls and the door were a mirage. There were no interruptions. Now away from everybody, except a few other men, Banerjee with the sun on his back applied paths of colour with his brush, observed it glisten and begin to dry, while his mind wandered without obstacles. As the sun went down, the pebbles and sticks at his feet each threw a shadow a mile long, and his own shape stretched into a ludicrous stick-insect, striding the earth—enough to make him wonder about himself.

Since their trip into town Banerjee joined the Americans at tea-breaks or after meals. To squat down without a word emphasised any familiarity. The Americans were relaxed about everything, including a world war. Their talk and attitudes were so easy Banerjee found himself only half-listening, in fact hardly at all. Without a word the pilot would get into the jeep, just for the hell of it, and chase kangaroos around the perimeter. A few times Banerjee and the pilot sat in the warm plane parked in the open hangar. When asked what exactly the plane was to be used for, the lanky American who was flicking switches and tapping instruments shrugged. 'Search me, my friend.'

In the few weeks that remained Banerjee formed a habit of

strolling down the runway after dark, joined by the camouflage officer who came alongside in his carpet slippers. With
hands clasped behind his back the officer recalled perfor-
mances at the Town Hall, the merits of different conductors
and pianists, but invariably turned to his wife and three
teenage daughters in Adelaide. 'Imagine,' he said, in mournful
affection, 'four women, under one roof.'

Banerjee had been receiving regular letters. Here were
trust and concern he could hold in his hand—words of almost
childlike roundness, beginning with the envelope. Willingly
his wife expressed more than he could ever manage. For her it
was like breathing. In reply he found there was little he could
say. Months apparently had passed. It came as a surprise or at
least was something to consider: what about him did she miss?

He mentioned to the officer, an older man, 'My wife, she
has written a letter—'

'Not bad news, I trust?'

'She tells me the front gate has come off its hinges. A little
thing. I mean, my wife would like me to be there now, this
minute, to fix it.'

The officer put his hand on Banerjee's shoulder. 'A woman
who misses you. The warmth in bed. There was symmetry, it
has been broken.' He coughed. 'The symmetry we enjoy so
much in music is illusion. That's my opinion.'

In the dark Banerjee found himself nodding. More and
more he was conscious of a slowness within, a holding-back,
as if he saw other people, even his own family, through pale-
blue eyes, whereas his were green-brown. Even if he wanted,
Banerjee could not be close. Not only to his wife but to all

other people, to things and events as well. It was as if the air was bent, holding him just away.

On the day in question the officer inspected the paint job from all angles, as the men waited. It took more than an hour. He came back, rubbing his hands. 'Well done. That should do the trick. Tomorrow we go on to the next.'

The Americans looking on had their arms folded.

'Only one way to test it.' The pilot put on his hat. 'You with me?'

Banerjee hadn't flown in a plane before. Soon the earth grew larger and the details smaller, reduced to casual marks, old worn patches, blobs of shadow. He twisted around to see the aerodrome. At this point the pilot tilted away and began diving; just for fun. He went low, then rose in a curve; Banerjee's stomach twisted and contracted. As always he composed his face.

Levelling out, the pilot now looked around for the aerodrome.

He gave a brief laugh. 'You sure as hell have done a job on the ground.'

Banerjee thought he saw wheel marks but it was nothing. The earth everywhere was the same—the same extensive dryness, one thing flowing into the next. When Banerjee turned and looked behind it was the same.

Climbing, the plane reached a point where it appeared to be staying in one spot, not making any progress. It was as if he was suspended above his own life. Looking down, as it were, he found he could not distinguish his life from the solid fact of the earth, which remained always below. He could not see what he had been doing there, moving about on it. Knees together, the dark hairs curving on the back of his hands.

Everything was clearer, yet not really. Plane's shadow: fleeting, religious. In the silence he was aware of his heartbeats, as if he hadn't noticed them before.

Now the earth in all its hardness and boulder unevenness came forward in a rush.

Briefly he wondered whether he—his life—could have turned out differently. Its many parts appeared to converge, in visibility later described as 'near perfect'.